ESCAPE TO FREEDOM

VANCY KASPER

AN IRWIN JUNIOR FICTION BOOK

First published in 1991 by
Stoddart Publishing Co. Limited
34 Lesmill Road
Toronto, Canada
M3B 2T6

Canadian Cataloguing in Publication Data

Kasper, Vancy
Escape to freedom

"Irwin Junior Fiction"
ISBN 0-7737-5452-0

I. Title

PS8571.A76E7 1991   C813'.54   C91-094938-7
PR9199.3.K37E7/1991

Cover Design: Brant Cowie / ArtPlus Limited
Cover Illustration: David Craig
Typesetting: Tony Gordon Ltd.

Printed and bound in Canada

For my sons,
Fred Kasper Jr. and Max Kasper

Although it is fiction, this book contains some
details of their father's life in Czechoslovakia
and Germany at the end of the Second World
War. I thank him for his love and support and
his unerring eye for those details, in spite of
horrible deprivation at the time.

Contents

Part I

FLIGHT
TO THE BORDER

1

Papa Has a Plan

*E*lsbeth scratched the red bites on her leg. It's my birthday, she said to herself. Her fingers probed, found the louse. Happy thirteenth birthday to me, she thought, thumb and finger squishing viciously. She swallowed the last of her tiny piece of bread. Gently she lifted a fold of skin hanging on her upper arm. Am I starving to death? she wondered.

"Drink *deinen kaffe*." Her mother's voice was low, her eyes greedy. Then she flushed and looked away. Her tone hardened but she continued, speaking German with the soft accent of Austrians living in Czechoslovakia. "We have to stay alive. Drink!"

Elsbeth barely heard her. In the distance she could glimpse the River Eger, dirty and wide as it crawled along. She felt strange.

"I ate my piece of bread, Mama. I'm okay. You take my coffee." Elsbeth held out the dappled blue enamel cup — but not so far out that some other woman could grab it. She saw the barbed wire reflected in her mother's eyes. Beyond her, five or six hundred women and children shuffled restlessly. Some sat. Some stood. But there was an uncertain swaying among them, like wind tossing a dried-out bunch of lifeless dirty clothes.

Her mother's hand shook across the distance between them. Roughly, she locked her fingers around the handle. She hardly looked at the cup as she gulped. Her eyes were never still. In fear, they flicked everywhere. Hello, barracks. Goodbye, parade ground. Good day, machine guns. Farewell, uniforms.

"Where's Emil? He should be back from the bathroom by now." A rare smile darted across Mama's face. This was a joke they both understood. The "bathroom" was an open trench behind a wall of boards.

"Happy birthday, *liebchen*." Mama's bony arm drew her close. "Papa has a plan," she whispered. "Do not worry. We'll get out of here."

Elsbeth stared. Was her mother beginning to crack? She had seen the wanderings and ravings of lots of women in the last two months. A plan? Papa was in a camp too. For men who didn't want to be communists. And he was over ten kilometres away. Worry began to hammer at Elsbeth. How could Mama know anything about Papa?

"I hear things," Mama continued. To Elsbeth, her eyes seemed alive with craziness. "A whisper here. A hint there." Catching the expression on her daughter's face, she laughed loudly. "When I march out of the camp with the others. You know, when the adults go to work in the factory. Papa is loved in Saaz. He gave work to so many people."

"Oh, Mama." Elsbeth hugged her. "Don't leave me. Don't go crazy like Frau Kasper." It's like hugging nothing but bones, she thought. She could see Emil threading his way back to them. He was limping.

"I'm hungry," he whined, picking at the bites on the back of his neck.

"Why are you limping?" Mama picked him up and sat him on her lap.

"A Czech boy threw a stone at me. I ran after him but a guard got mad at us."

"Haven't we had enough? We survive Hitler and his Gestapo. Now when we're supposed to be free, we end up in a camp." Mama's hatred filled her voice and eyes as she stared at the guards. "Why did the Americans withdraw? Why did they let the Russians and those crazy Czech communists take over? We don't even know them! They come from Russia and throw us in here!" Finally her voice broke. "The war ended four months ago, God give us grace."

Elsbeth touched her mother's cheek. "Please, Mama. Don't. You said we had a plan?"

"A plan?" Emil's head swivelled instantly. He sucked his cheeks in and spat in the dirt.

"Keep quiet, *dumkopf*. You'll get us all shot."

"Hush, Elsbeth. You are a big boy, Emil. Act like one. Seven-year-old boys know when to keep their mouths shut." Like moths fluttering, Mama's hands flew to her son's head. "Your hair. It's filthy. Today when you children are roaming the country-side, look for apples. But eat them very slowly. You'll get cramps if you don't. I'll see you back here after work."

Off in the distance, Elsbeth could see Russian soldiers taking apart abandoned cars. The pieces would be shipped home. Elsbeth knew the Russians were clever at rebuilding stuff. Papa had told her. They dismantled everything. Even flush toilets from empty houses were sent on the train, home to Russia.

Her mother's voice sounded weaker these days. "Elsbeth is the boss. Always do what Elsbeth says." She gave Emil a loving shake as he stuck his tongue out at his sister. "Do you understand?" They both struggled to stand up. "Come. It's time to line up and be counted. Remember now, don't wander too far through the fields. I'll see you tonight."

"I know," Emil mimicked Mama's high-pitched voice. *"Papa has a plan."*

"Shut up, you little twerp." Elsbeth wished she could get rid of Emil. She wanted to find her very own dog. Run with a dog for a while. Forget about dreams of creamy torte cake. Escape from the machine-gun fire that dotted their days and nights. Forget the story of a distant aunt's house near the German border exploding in a million pieces; the tale of her cousin's hand sticking up through bits of flowered wallpaper. They had been lucky in Saaz. Only two bombs had fallen here.

They walked across the compound and lined up with the others in rows of six across. They waited for their names to be called.

The count had just begun when a Czech communist soldier spoke to Mama. "Hildegarde Hoffer? Come with me. There is mail for you."

"Mail? But nobody ever gets mail in here!" Terrified, Mama pushed Elsbeth and Emil behind her. The other women in line shivered. Furtively they drew their own children close.

"Hail Mary, full of grace . . . ," chanted one of them.

"Follow me, I said!" The guard gestured with his rifle.

"Take care of Emil, Elsbeth." Mama's voice broke as she turned to go.

"We're coming with you. We're not staying here. Come on, Emil!" Elsbeth grabbed her brother and ran after Mama.

Mama turned, tears streaming down her face. She hesitated. There was a sharp click as the guard unlocked the safety catch on the rifle. With a gasp, Mama grabbed each child by the hand. "Come on, then. If we have to die, we'll die together."

Elsbeth knew, as they trudged out through the front gate, that they might not die. That was what Mama was afraid of. What happened before the dying. She'd heard the screams. She knew what they meant. She kept watching her mother, whose lips were moving silently.

"Get in." The guard had stopped in front of a car.

Mama pushed the two of them into the back seat ahead of her. She was frowning. Elsbeth could feel her confusion. Why would they be riding in a car? They should have been made to walk. Elsbeth gave her mother's hand a little squeeze.

They drove over streets paved with cobblestones into Saaz. Elsbeth stretched, trying to see her own home, but the car was moving too fast. Finally the guard pulled up in front of the ancient town hall. Elsbeth struggled to breathe. Saaz had been built hundreds of years ago. She knew there were musty jail cells in the basement of this building.

The guard herded them out of the car, up the front steps. Emil twisted this way, looking at all the khaki uniforms, that way at carts drawn by old horses.

Upstairs, the guard flung open the door to a large office. "Captain Jindrich, here is Hildegarde Hoffer." He pushed the three of them into the room and left, closing the door behind him.

"Herr Jindrich!" Elsbeth felt like dancing. Sitting behind a huge desk was the former manager of Papa's factory. "It's Herr Jindrich!" She smiled and started towards him. But Emil, like a cannonball, shot past her and hurled himself onto Herr Jindrich's lap. His fingers were greedy as they opened pockets, looking for candy.

"Sorry, son. No candy today." Herr Jindrich gave Emil an almost embarrassed hug.

Mama said nothing. Elsbeth was halfway across the room when she became aware of the silence behind her. She stopped and turned to face her mother. The stark terror on her mother's face shocked her. Confused, she whirled back to stare at Herr Jindrich. Then she saw the Red Star. Right in the middle of the desk. And she saw the red epaulettes on the shoulders of his uniform.

Herr Jindrich was a *commissar!* The boss of the Secret Police. Their former manager had become the most feared person in Saaz. He was the local arm of the dreaded KGB.

"We have little time, Frau Hoffer. Sit down." He placed Emil firmly on the floor, then went and locked the office door. He lowered his voice as he picked up some documents. "Here are identity papers. I've had them stamped by the Russians." He rummaged on the other side of the desk and held out some money. "A hundred koruna will buy railway tickets and get you across the border into Bayreuth."

Elsbeth gasped. "That's where the Americans are. Across No Man's Land. That's five hundred kilometres away!"

"Be quiet!" He tilted his head, listening, then continued. "I've seen your husband, Frau Hoffer. He'll get out through the Russian zone into Bavaria. But wait for him at Bayreuth. Hide these." He folded Mama's fingers around the papers. "Tomorrow you leave the camp in the morning. You will not return."

"This is a trick! I don't believe you!"

"Frau Hoffer, I had to take this job. They said they'd deport me if I didn't. To Russia. They want a Czech commissar here. Now my own country-men don't trust me." He began to pace back and forth. "I was never that much of a communist. I could fail at this job. That puts me and my son at risk. He's all I've got. I don't want my son being shipped off to Russia. *Jaroslav goes out with you.* He will meet you tomorrow by the old blacksmith's shop, just outside town. That's the deal."

Mama looked so vulnerable that Herr Jindrich smiled at her. "How does Canada sound to you?" Her eyes filled with tears. He squeezed her hand, then went to unlock the door. "Go now. The car will take you back to the camp. Keep the money hidden. Emil! Elsbeth! Remember now, tell no one!"

Walking back through the camp gates, Mama was dazed. The guards had shunted a train into the camp. Soldiers were milling everywhere, but she hardly saw them. She had given the money and papers to Elsbeth. "Use that safety pin you found. Pin them to your underwear. I might be searched today at the factory, who knows?" Her whole face lit up as she grabbed and hugged the two of them. "Tomorrow we'll be free. Hush now."

The roll call was still going on. Just as the three of them walked to the back of the lines, soldiers approached. They began pulling screaming women out of the lines.

All the blood seemed to drain from Mama's face. Her hand flew to her heart. She stumbled as a guard yanked her arm and dragged her out of her place in line, up to the front.

The doors of the train slid open. The women were forced in.

Elsbeth heard moans and sobbing all around her. Mama was on her way to Russia. To a labour camp.

2

Three Small Villages Away

I'm the boss, Jaroslav."

"I know, I know." Herr Jindrich's son kicked viciously at a large stone. "Just don't push me, okay?"

Elsbeth stared at Jaroslav, trying to figure him out. His expression, the arrogant thrust of his shoulders reminded her of the guards at the camp. He could be trouble, she thought.

Her silence seemed to upset him. "I said goodbye to my father last night. So let's get on with this," he snapped. But his voice broke as he turned away and Elsbeth was sure he was struggling not to cry. "He said that from now on I need you and you need me."

She knelt on the ground behind the old smithy. With a stick she drew the road to Eger in the dirt. She felt sorry for Jaroslav, but she'd learned in the camp not to trust anyone too quickly.

"Who knows, maybe my father can get away. Maybe I'll see him in Bayreuth." Jaroslav's pain etched every word.

"Maybe. But look here. We have to go past these three villages to get to Kaarlsbaad. There's a friend of my father's there — we call him Uncle Moritz." She stood up and faced Herr Jindrich's son. "Since you're Czech, you'll have to do all the talking." She put her arm around her brother. "Do you understand, Emil? Not one word. People would recognize our Austrian accents and report us."

Emil showed no sign of having heard. It probably didn't matter. He had gone so far inside himself that maybe he would never come out. He hadn't uttered a word since Mama was taken away.

The sound of a milk cart, rumbling wooden wheels over stones, made them flatten themselves against the building. Elsbeth and Jaroslav exchanged frightened glances.

"We should walk alongside," Elsbeth hissed as it came closer. "We have to look busy. Unless we're obviously hunting for food or doing a job, the police will pick us up."

Listening to herself, Elsbeth wondered who she was. Someone not quite as frozen as Emil. But it didn't sound like her own voice. She couldn't worry about things like that right now, she told herself.

"No one's going to pick us up, we're only kids. The whole country's full of kids roaming around in the daytime." Jaroslav slouched, hands in his pockets. He wrinkled his nose. "You two smell."

"Shut up, Jaroslav. You can stay if you want to, but we're leaving. Come on, Emil." Elsbeth dragged Emil off to join up with the cart as it passed the alleyway. Jaroslav wiped out the map with his boot and ran after them.

Clip clop. Clip clop. The old horse moved slowly. The farmer hadn't noticed them. They hung towards the back, their hands on the milk cans. Elsbeth's mouth watered when she saw a long white bag hanging from a front door. She knew it was waiting for chewy fresh bagels to be dropped in it. But the town baker had been killed at the front lines in 1943.

"Good day." The farmer greeted the policeman who stood in the middle of the road. *"Tsk tsk,"* he clicked to stop his horse.

"You're an old geezer to have such young children, aren't you?" The policeman pointed. Jaroslav nervously moved one of the milk cans. Elsbeth grabbed Emil and sat him up on the cart as if he belonged.

"Eh? Eh? You'll have to speak louder." The farmer hadn't even seen them.

"I said who are . . . " He was interrupted by yelling. Across the large square, two civilians, probably Czech communists, were trying to subdue a young man. The policeman dropped the bridle and ran to assist them.

"We've got to get away from here right now!" Elsbeth hissed as she lifted Emil off the cart. They darted into another alleyway and immediately slowed down to a walk. She and Jaroslav knew they couldn't risk drawing attention to themselves. Emil just followed like some mindless machine. Elsbeth wondered if he'd ever come to life again.

"Wait a minute." Elsbeth halted. "How are we going to get through town now? We've got to go back. Maybe that farmer will help us."

"We can't trust him." Jaroslav pointed to Emil's prison armband. "We were lucky the policeman didn't see those. Then he'd know you and your brother were from the camp and not the farmer's children."

They leaned up against the crumbling mortar to think. Elsbeth knew they had to leave their armbands on until they got out of town. They would be in even more danger without them. Saaz was a small place and the townsfolk whose families had lived there for generations might recognize them as Austrians. But with their armbands they were relatively safe as long as they looked busy. Everyone knew the camp kids were free to roam for food and help with odd jobs.

"We could say we're going to move apples in a cart."

"With you along, Jaroslav, it's hard. Everyone knows you're Herr Jindrich's son. No one would ever believe that you were going to work with prisoners."

"You're right. Wait a minute! I could say my father ordered me to help. I could tell them he wants me to be busy."

Elsbeth frowned and scratched her arm. "I still think it would be best if we caught up to that farmer.

He's probably going right through town to the next village."

Jaroslav shrugged. "Maybe."

"If we're stopped again, we could use your story about the apples." Yells from the town square drifted down the alley. "Come on. The police are still busy with that man, and the farmer probably kept on going. This is our chance."

They ran back. Elsbeth had been right. Everyone in a uniform was across the square. Hearts pounding, they sauntered by. A few blocks later, they caught up with the cart and again sheltered themselves behind it.

Soon they had left the gaunt faces of the townsfolk behind and were walking along a gravel road, under oak trees. Acorns had dropped and the leaves were already a burnished red. Around the bend up ahead, Elsbeth could hear the dull thud of a pick hitting the earth.

She lifted Emil onto the cart. "Jaroslav," she said in a low voice. "Go round to the back of the cart. Those workers up ahead might recognize you." The locals were busy with shovels and wheelbarrows repairing the road.

"You and Emil better take off those armbands now," Jaroslav said. "Anyone sees them out here and back you'll go to prison."

Elsbeth picked at her armband. The joy of seeing Herr Jindrich, the horror of Mama being dragged away shrieking, all that seemed to have happened a long time ago. She knew her strength was waning, that she was on the edge of giving up. She took off Emil's armband. Funny the farmer hasn't turned around once, she thought. Without armbands on, we look as if we're part of his family. Her spirits lifted a little. He can't betray us if he doesn't even know we're here.

They were moving closer and closer to the work crew. Kaarlsbaad was only three small villages away, but it felt as remote as India. Would the workmen challenge them? The nerve along Elsbeth's shoulder twinged. She hoped Jaroslav had the sense to bend down and pretend to be examining the underside of the cart.

"Good day." The farmer tipped his cap as the workmen parted to let him by. One of them, wearing the torn, dirty uniform of a war veteran, stared suspiciously at Elsbeth. Her grip on Emil tightened, although she knew her brother would sit like a stone. She held her breath. These returned soldiers often went a little crazy as they tried to fit into a way of life that was gone. They could be dangerous.

She let her breath go only when she heard the thud of the pick again, this time hitting stone. Jaroslav came around the cart to walk with her, and they plodded on as the road meandered towards the first small village.

"We've got to get something to eat," Elsbeth gasped as her toe hit a stone and she stumbled. "I'm feeling funny."

"Maybe we can get an egg in the next village."

"No. Someone might report us. Let's go over that hill. The one up ahead." She pointed.

As they reached the curve in the road, Elsbeth saw the statue of a saint. "Now," she said. "I know the way. We'll come back down to the road beyond the village." Silently asking the saint for help, she lifted Emil off the cart and they began their climb.

Halfway up, Elsbeth turned to find the farmer staring at them. She stared back. Is he winking at us? she thought. Now *I'm* going crazy. She pulled Emil after her as they went over the crest of the hill.

"There's an apple tree over there," Jaroslav whooped and ran off. Elsbeth's legs gave out and she collapsed. She waited while he wrestled with the branches, reaching higher and higher. There's got to be one or two no one has found, she prayed.

Back he came, grinning. Elsbeth reached eagerly for the apple he held out, but when she bit into it she gagged, feeling sick. She took a deep breath and swallowed a tiny bit. She waited. With a sigh of relief, she knew it would stay down. She passed it to Emil. He ignored it.

Terrified, Elsbeth suddenly slapped him, hard. "Eat. You must eat. Or you'll die." She slapped him again, feeling hysteria shoot through her body. Emil stared straight ahead. Elsbeth slapped him again.

"Eeeeeeeeee!" The shriek, full of anguish, almost scorched the meadow. Emil hurled his arms around Elsbeth's neck, crying, "Mama, Mama, Mama," over and over.

Elsbeth held him, tears running down her own face. She rocked him back and forth. Jaroslav kicked hard at a stone, then walked a little distance away to keep a lookout.

"Listen, Emil. We're going to meet Papa. In Bayreuth. So eat, little Emil. Eat. You want to see Papa, don't you?"

"I want Mama."

Crying and holding him tight, Elsbeth stammered, "We can't talk about Mama anymore. She's gone. Far away to a labour camp."

Emil wriggled back and hiccupped. "Will we ever see her again?"

"I don't know. Nobody knows. But you and me and Jaroslav have to meet Papa." She tilted her brother's chin up and looked into his eyes. "Remember how Papa taught you to whistle, Emil? Remember? Well, we'll all be whistling as soon as we get across the border. And Papa says we're all going far across the ocean to Canada."

"But you've got to keep your mouth shut, Emil." Jaroslav had come back to kneel down beside them. "It's a secret. An important secret. We could die if you tell." He ate half the second apple and passed it to Emil, who took his first bite of food since the previous morning.

"What we need is a good horse," Jaroslav muttered, stretching out on the grass.

Elsbeth stared at him. "Wait a minute." She jumped up and twirled around. "I know where we can find a horse. A strong horse. A great horse!" Dizzy, she fell back on the grass, laughing. "A wonderful horse to ride through Kaarlsbaad all the way to Eger." Laughing and rolling on the grass, she added hysterically, "That's where the border is."

Jaroslav was looking at her as if she had gone crazy. He took a step or two back.

Giggling and hiccupping, she forced herself to calm down. She took another careful bite of the apple. Then another. When she had finished it, she continued.

"I'm not crazy. Honest. I know where we can steal a horse." She twisted around. "But we have to head back a little bit till we reach the river again."

"Okay, okay. But we've got to get food more often. You're acting as if you're someplace else all the time." Elsbeth nodded, realizing that she had scared him. Serves him right, she thought. He'd been well fed all along. Didn't he realize that she and Emil had been slowly starving for months?

They set off over the hills. Elsbeth shivered in the fall air and tried to walk faster. They were careful to avoid the small stone and brick houses with their tiny windows. Finally, crossing a field, Elsbeth spotted the River Eger ahead of them. She pointed over to her left. "There it is! A whole island full of horses."

3

Stealing a Horse

*L*ook at that big black one!" Jaroslav pointed. "He's the one I want." Down below, grazing in the meadow, wandering through the woods, drinking at the pond, were horses of all colours and sizes. "There's so many! There must be two hundred of them. Elsbeth, how did you know about these horses?"

"Here, horsy. Here, horsy," Emil called. Skipping and half falling, he raced down the hill. Running after him, watching his legs pump below his short pants, Elsbeth smiled. Now all she'd have to worry about was him keeping his mouth shut.

"Ask me no questions, I'll tell you no lies," she called back over her shoulder. She didn't want to share with anyone the secret of how this island had been her special place before the war, how it had nurtured her, how safe she had felt here.

During recent months she had come here for

apples to take back to the camp. She remembered the many times she had watched, hidden in the underbrush, while two men rounded up the horses and counted them every afternoon. Right now, she and Emil and Jaroslav were safe. The guards were lazy. They camped over on the far side of the island and never came around to this side until roundup time. But she knew it wouldn't do to linger.

Down the hill they ran until they arrived panting at the shore. They stared across at the huge island. Sluggish and muddy, the Eger parted to flow around it. The grass and water were struck with the crystal light of fall. Clouds tumbled across the sky like wild cotton balls.

"We'll never get them across." Jaroslav hurled a stone viciously towards the water. "How can we even get there in the first place? We could swim, I guess. But it would take years for our clothes to dry. You're so thin, you'd get pneumonia for sure." He hurled another stone that skipped — one, two, three. "Anyway, we'd have to leave Emil behind. He might wander off somewhere. We'd never find him."

"It's okay. See that little piece of land jutting out?" Elsbeth pointed. "We can walk across from there. Come on; I'll show you." She beckoned, and the two of them followed her. She led them around the curve of the water and out onto the spit. "Just follow me."

"No. I'm not going. I can't swim that well." Jaroslav sat down on a rock. "Emil can't swim either, I bet."

"We can walk right across! There's a ford here. It only goes to our knees until we're almost at the island. Then it's only a little deeper. We'll be fine. I used to walk across all the time."

"Why don't the horses run across then, if it's so easy?"

Impatient with the two of them, Emil had already begun tiny forays out into the water, skipping stones.

"Emil! Wait. Take off your shoes and stockings and carry them." Elsbeth's tone was sharp. "You've got to follow right behind me or you could slip off into deeper water." She bent over and picked up her own leather shoes. "Come on, Jaroslav."

Holding Emil by the hand, she led the way very slowly. Sure enough, the water didn't even reach her knees. She stopped about a hundred metres from a sandy beach scattered with stones and boulders. "Hold on tight, it gets a little deeper here." Carefully she placed one foot in front of the other until all three of them felt the river bed rise again. Finally they wiggled their toes against the warm sand.

"I wonder where that black one is." Jaroslav wandered towards the brush.

"Wait!" Elsbeth sat down and dried her feet against the hem of her skirt. "I know which horse will be easy to catch. We're not taking three horses. We're just going to take one."

"One horse! Are you crazy? We'll never get to Bayreuth! We need three horses!" Suddenly

Jaroslav stomped off. "I'm sick of you telling us what to do all the time."

"I got you to the island, didn't I? You were ready to give up." Elsbeth felt giddy again. She couldn't put her energy into fighting. "Three horses would be reported. One could have just strayed off."

Jaroslav sulked as he listened to her. "I don't even know why I'm here." His voice rose. "I don't want to go anywhere with you. I don't want to leave my father. You're supposed to need me, but you don't care about anything I say."

"That's not true, Jaroslav. We do need you. You're Czech. If Emil or I even open our mouths, we'll give ourselves away. We'll be arrested. We'll be sent *back*. Do you know what that means? We'll *die*." She took a deep breath. "You've got to do all our talking for us until we get to the border."

She walked over to him. In spite of herself she began to tremble. "We really need you. You don't know what the camp is like." Terror surged through her. "You'd be lucky. All that would happen to you is that you'd be taken back to your father. They wouldn't even know you'd done anything wrong." She turned away from him, struggling to fight the hopelessness that washed over her.

"How can one horse help us?" He kicked hard at a stone. Then he muttered, "I mustn't be caught either. They'd blame my father. He'd be killed."

"One horse won't be noticed. If the three of us ride him, anyone who sees us will think we're from a farm. We won't be challenged so easily. We can go across the fields instead of having to stick so close to the roads." Elsbeth twirled around clapping her hands. "This horse will get us to Kaarlsbaad. There's an old man there. He's a friend of my father's. I told you about him already. He'll buy our tickets for us. Then we can go by train to the border."

"Why don't we ride the horse all the way to the border?" Then, without waiting for her to answer, he held out his hand. "Okay, Elsbeth. We have a bargain. Let's shake on it. I'll do the talking. You do the navigating." He smiled. "We've got to keep changing vehicles, don't we? Otherwise those Czech communists will catch us. Right?"

"Right." Elsbeth felt her knees almost buckle. Thank Mary, Mother of God, that she and Jaroslav would be standing together from now on. She shook his hand hard, up and down, for emphasis. "We have a bargain. Now let's look for that horse I saw the last time I was here. She's friendly and gentle. A dappled brown. The three of us should be able to get her."

After putting their shoes back on, they plunged into the underbrush. It was a bit swampy and the cat-tails were swollen and brown, ripe for picking. Emil reached for some berries and was about to eat them.

"*Don't.*" Elsbeth grabbed them out of his hand. At her yell, a horse that had been standing under a tree bolted. "This is deadly nightshade, Emil." She hurled them down. "There's a tree that has those brown apples somewhere around here. As soon as we have you up on the horse, I'll get us some apples."

As they walked along, by now approaching a deeper forest, Elsbeth searched the ground. The horses had been here for months, so she knew she'd find some leather thonging or a piece of rope to help them.

"Here it is! Here's the length of rope we need." She turned back to Jaroslav, who was following behind. "How do you think we should round her up?"

He thought a minute. "First of all, we should get the apples now. We can put them in our pockets. The horses we've passed trot off as soon as we get close. So if she doesn't want to come, Emil can offer her an apple and you and I can come up from either side."

Elsbeth nodded and changed direction. "The apple tree's at the edge of the next clearing. We'd better get a drink at the pond over here first. The water's brackish, but it's a lot better than river water. River water makes you sick."

After they'd had a drink and found the apple tree, they both turned to Emil. "Up at the very top," Elsbeth pointed. "See? Along those thin branches? They must be the only ones the horses didn't already get. Come on, I'll give you a boost."

Emil's leather shoes slipped once or twice on the shiny bark. Elsbeth's mouth was watering. Her stomach was empty again. Emil shook the branches above him.

"Look out! Here they come!"

Jaroslav caught one or two as they dropped. Elsbeth picked another three from the ground.

They were tiny and slightly bitter, but they were safe to eat.

"We'll share two of them. Just two. We have to keep the others for our ride." She took a small bite and chewed slowly. Emil clambered down with another apple, already bitten into, in his hand. "Good work, *liebchen*." Elsbeth patted him on the shoulder, then studied the horses standing nearby.

One of them, a dappled brown, trotted up to her and nuzzled at her hand. "Here she is. Take it easy now. Jaroslav, you put the rope around her neck. Emil, you climb up onto her."

Emil was jumping up and down. "Give me a boost, Jaroslav."

Having slipped the rope over the horse's neck, Jaroslav did just that.

"Now how do *we* get up?"

"Lead her to that rock over there. We can stand on it and get on."

"This horse is tame. I wonder who owns all these horses." He held the rope while Elsbeth jumped on in front of Emil.

"The Russian Army, that's who," she called over her shoulder to him as he mounted the rump.

"The Russian Army! You mean we're stealing a Russian horse?"

"That's right. Don't worry about it — I've never seen the guards on this side of the island at this time of day. We have to get to Kaarlsbaad. That's all that counts." Elsbeth click-clicked her tongue, and the horse walked steadily through the woods, back the way they'd come.

"Come on, horsy. Come on, horsy," chanted Emil, stuck between the two of them.

When they reached the beach, the horse stopped. Elsbeth patted her neck and pressed her flanks, urging her to step into the water.

Very slowly the horse put one leg in, then another, then began tentatively to cross the ford. Finally they began to come up onto the shallower part and Elsbeth patted her again.

"Wheeoueet!" The whistle shot out from the shore and immediately the horse wheeled around. Stumbling a little, she walked back to the island, whinnying as she went.

Elsbeth's hand flew to her throat. Emil peered around her and his arms tightened around her waist.

Jaroslav moaned, "I'm scared. What do we do now?"

There, waiting on the rocky beach, was the fiercest-looking man they'd ever seen. Long, greasy black hair and a large curling moustache set off a tough, tanned face and piercing, slanted eyes. He cracked his whip against the stones, lightly, as if playing with it.

"Look at his eyes! Look at his face! He's going to whip us!" Emil started to cry.

"Jaroslav! You do all the talking. Talk Russian. You must know some, it's so close to Czech." Elsbeth's heart was beating wildly. "He's a Mongol. From beyond the Ural Mountains. I heard them talking once. You know, a Tartar." She squeezed Emil's hand. "Hush now, *liebchen.*"

"Taking my horse for some exercise, were you?" The man squinted up at them.

"Yes," stammered Jaroslav. "We thought we could get some apples that are farther away if we had a horse," he added in stumbling Russian. Then in a low voice, he mumbled, "We're hungry."

The man stared at them. Then, from the pocket of his leather tunic, he drew a huge piece of salami. "Hungry, eh? Better get down and have a piece of this." He lifted a snivelling Emil down first, then Elsbeth. Jaroslav jumped off himself.

Elsbeth couldn't take her eyes off the salami. She and Emil had had nothing but bread and watery soup for the last five months. Before that it hadn't been much better. They'd had meat only two or three times since the war began.

From out of one leather boot, the soldier drew a knife. He cut three large hunks of salami and gave one to each of the children. Elsbeth held her piece to her nose. She felt faint from the wonderful smell of it. Then she forced herself to chew very slowly, so she wouldn't vomit it all up later. She poked Emil and bent to whisper in his ear. "Slow. Chew it slowly."

The Tartar was watching her. "Why doesn't she speak?" he demanded.

"She's shy. And Papa said not to talk to strangers."

The soldier suddenly threw back his head and laughed. "Mine too, and I tell my children that." He sat down and invited them to sit beside him.

Jaroslav told her later what the Tartar had said.

He explained that he was very attached to all the horses on the island. He had been with them so long, through so many battles, that he knew every single one of them. His own horse, Wheat Rustling in the Wind, had been with him since the beginning. He had never had one holiday. Now he was longing to be shipped home, back to the Ural Mountains.

"My wife and children are waiting," he finished in a low voice. Without another word, he cut off another piece of salami and held it out to Jaroslav. Then he got up and walked away, the horse following.

Still chewing on her salami, Elsbeth was puzzled. She was used to thinking of the Russian soldiers as ogres, and this one looked so fierce. Yet he had been so kind.

She sighed and sneaked a glance at Jaroslav. He puzzled her too. She didn't know how much to trust him. He'd never been in a camp or gone without any food at all for eight whole days as she had. But this time he'd kept his head. He hadn't panicked. She was thankful for that. And she was glad to have someone older with her to help with Emil. She stood up, wiping her hands on her smock.

"Come on. Let's take off our shoes and get back to the mainland. It's a long walk to Kaarlsbaad and Uncle Moritz."

4

Terror in the Forest

*T*he meat Elsbeth had eaten danced through her muscles. The pungent odour of just harvested hops still lingered on the air, and even that made her smile as she led the way to the east. She refused to think about the days it would take to walk the 145 kilometres from Saaz to Kaarlsbaad or worry about whether the leather in their shoes would last. We must have gone about twenty kilometres already, she thought. We're on our way!

Jaroslav and Emil fooled around behind her. Elsbeth's heart sang as she heard Emil giggling. But she kept a sharp lookout as they wended their way through a field of dried-out corn husks. She knew that each farmer in the tiny villages might have as many as twenty hectares, but they would not be lumped together. There would be one field here, then another maybe ten kilometres away. So there was always a chance of being seen, and she didn't trust Jaroslav to be watchful.

"Where are we going, anyway?" Jaroslav caught up to her just as they entered a forest.

"We're following the River Eger," Elsbeth said crisply as she looked around. "It'll take us right to Kaarlsbaad."

"Can't catch me!" Emil yelled and tore ahead.

"*Gggggrrrrrrr!*"

Elsbeth and Jaroslav froze as a wild boar sprang out of the underbrush, landing between them and Emil. Emil looked back and his mouth fell open. Head down, fangs dripping, the boar pawed the ground in warning.

"Get . . . up . . . the . . . nearest . . . tree . . . Emil." Elsbeth kept her voice very quiet. "But don't make any sudden moves." Behind her Jaroslav backed slowly away to a nearby tree and then scrambled up to a low branch. Keeping her eye on the animal, Elsbeth too began to back up very slowly. Across the distance beyond the boar, Emil, white-faced, edged towards a tree.

With a horrible grunting noise, the boar charged at Emil. Shrieking, the boy frantically clambered up the trunk just as Elsbeth's foot struck against a sturdy branch that lay on the ground.

Rage filled her. "Leave my brother alone!" she screamed, picking up the branch. Surprised, the boar halted and wheeled to face her. The grunting and squealing rose in crescendo. Elsbeth brandished her weapon. "Come on . . . you . . . you stupid . . ."

"Elsbeth. Don't be crazy! He'll gore you!" Jaroslav started down the tree.

Ignoring him, Elsbeth faced the boar. Every growl the wild pig made, Elsbeth growled back. Suddenly the snarling boar leaped for her throat, fangs bared. Flexing her muscles as hard as she could, Elsbeth crashed the heavy stave across the boar's skull. The animal stopped in midair and dropped with a heavy thud. Elsbeth flung the stave away and started up the nearest tree.

All three of them stared wide-eyed at the animal lying beneath them. Slowly the boar opened its eyes, bent its front legs and staggered to its feet. Shaking its head, it trotted off, stumbling a little every now and then.

"Wow!" Emil was staring in admiration at Elsbeth. "You saved my life."

"Let's get out of this forest, fast." Jaroslav swung his legs out to jump down.

"No! Wait a while. It might come back." Elsbeth felt so weak, she didn't know if she could ever walk again.

They sat clinging to the branches for what seemed like years. At last, watchfully, they climbed down. When Elsbeth felt the ground, firm beneath her feet, she almost fell.

"We can't walk to Kaarlsbaad. It's too far and it's too dangerous." Jaroslav turned to face the way they'd come. "We've got to try that road we saw when we crossed the cornfield."

"No. We could be picked up by the police."

"You almost got yourself killed anyway. We're

tired and it's getting dark. We've got to get a ride."
Jaroslav strode off.

"I'm scared. I want to see Uncle Moritz right
now!" Emil's determined little body followed after
him. "Come on, Elsbeth."

Elsbeth held back for a moment, then with a
shuddering look over her shoulder, she ran after
them.

They trudged along the road in the long fall dusk.
Elsbeth was exhausted now, but she wasn't hungry.
The meat was still nourishing her. She needn't have
worried about being seen. They met no one, and
the only thing that broke the silence was the hawk-
ing cry of scavenger crows.

Darkness had finally fallen when Emil dropped
down at the edge of the road.

"I'm tired. I want to go to sleep." He lay back
and closed his eyes.

"Don't be silly, Emil." Elsbeth pulled at his arm,
trying to get him back on his feet. "We've got to
keep going. Uncle Moritz is waiting."

"Come on, Elsbeth. I'm tired too. Let's rest for
a while." Jaroslav plunked himself down on a
boulder and pulled a blade of field grass to draw
back and forth between his teeth.

Elsbeth stared down at both of them. The ground
seemed to reach up and pull her down, down, to
enfold her in its arms. She collapsed between them.

Elsbeth woke up shivering, disturbed by the rumble of what sounded like a truck coming closer and
closer. Framed in the bright headlights, Jaroslav

was standing in the middle of the road, waving his arms over his head.

"Emil! Wake up! We might have to run." She shook her brother, who sat up yawning and rubbing his eyes. "Jaroslav! Get out of sight! There could be Czech communists in that truck."

"You took a chance with the boar. I'm taking a chance with the truck." Jaroslav kept on waving.

Stupid fool, Elsbeth thought, searching the darkness behind them for some place to hide quickly.

"Wait a minute, Elsbeth. The truck sounds like an Opel. It could be carrying machinery."

The truck came to a noisy halt, and the driver leaned out the window. Blond hair framed a surly face.

"Yeah? What's the trouble?"

"The boy," Jaroslav answered back in Czech, pointing to Emil. "He's sick. We've got to get him to Kaarlsbaad."

"Kaarlsbaad. Kaarlsbaad. That's all I hear from morning to night. Get enough gas to get to Kaarlsbaad. Get the winnowing equipment to Kaarlsbaad. The foreman acts like he's going to get shot if I don't get the stuff to Kaarlsbaad." The man studied the three of them. "Who's the girl?"

Elsbeth opened her mouth to answer, then clamped her lips shut.

"My sister. She's deaf. She can't speak."

"Yeah, well she moved her lips right then."

"She saw your lips moving, that's all. Please give us a ride."

Smoke from the driver's cigarette floated in the

uneasy silence surrounding them. Tears crept down Emil's cheeks, and grabbing Elsbeth, he buried his face in her skirt, sobbing.

"All right, all right. Tell the kid to stop blubbering. Heard enough of that in the war. Get in the back with the machinery. The little guy can lie down back there." He turned the key in the ignition and the engine rumbled over as they walked to the back of the truck. "It's a long trip and I ain't got no food. So don't ask me for none."

Jaroslav hauled open the doors and helped Elsbeth and Emil into the truck. Then he jumped up and managed to swing one leg in. Elsbeth dragged the rest of him in and they both fell back on the floor.

"Okay," Jaroslav yelled.

The driver revved up the engine, and the truck coughed and sputtered its swaying way along the road. Elsbeth drew Emil closer to her as the cold seeped into her bones. Even Jaroslav huddled up against them as one hour, then another slowly passed.

The two boys fell asleep again, but Elsbeth was too cold. She felt for the safety pin. Relief passed through her — the papers and the money were still there. With those, Papa's friend Uncle Moritz could buy train tickets to Eger for them. Once over the mountains and across the border, they would be with Papa again. She smiled, even though her teeth were chattering. Her stockings were light, and she envied Emil and Jaroslav, whose heavier ones covered their legs right up to their knickerbockers.

Up front, the driver honked every now and then, and Elsbeth knew that workers who lived in the countryside must be bicycling home even this late. The sweetness of sugar beets hung on the night air. It was beet harvest time for the farmers.

Jaroslav and Emil woke up as the truck slowed down and finally stopped. Elsbeth stretched and began hopping up and down to get warm.

Jaroslav opened the back doors. "We're in Kaarlsbaad. Yippee!" He waved towards the street and the clustered houses. Candles were shining through the windows of a small church. He jumped out onto the road and held up his arms for Emil, who pushed him away.

"I can jump out myself."

Elsbeth put her hands on Jaroslav's shoulders and swung down to stand beside them.

The driver's voice floated back through the dark night. "You better know where you're going. There's a curfew here too." He shifted gears and stepped on the accelerator, and the truck rumbled away, leaving them staring after it.

Elsbeth walked to the nearest corner and strained to see the name of the street. She knew Kaarlsbaad was about the same size as Saaz. "We'd better walk for a while, till I see something familiar," she whispered.

"There are some soldiers. Way over there." Jaroslav pointed and the three of them slunk against a wall. "You'd better find something fast."

They edged their way along for a few minutes, until at last they came to a square Elsbeth recognized. She paused, trying to get herself oriented.

"This way." Elsbeth turned right, then left, then right again, praying she'd remembered the route.

She had. "This is the street." Her voice shook with relief. "Uncle Moritz lives at number 18."

When they reached the ancient door of number 18, Elsbeth knocked loudly. Her heart was racing. At last they were safe. At last someone would look after them. She craned her neck to see through the ill-fitting window to one side.

"There's isn't even a candle," Jaroslav said as they stood waiting. Finally, he set off down the side alley to the back of the house.

Elsbeth felt the hand of fear grip her heart. Had Uncle Moritz been taken like Papa? Was he in a camp too? Even though he was Czech, he wasn't a communist.

Suddenly a neighbour flung open her door and called out, "What do you want there?"

"We've come to see her uncle." Jaroslav, who had run back, pointed at Elsbeth.

"Oh, well, if he's your uncle, I guess it's all right for you children to walk in. Just lift the latch and call out. The old man is probably sleeping. He's been sick for two weeks now. Can't even get up from his bed. The doctor was killed in the war and we haven't called the priest yet. But between you and me, the last rites are not far off."

5

Setback

"*U*ncle Moritz?" Holding a lighted candle, Elsbeth bent over the wasted body, yellowing in its fight for life. The man's sour breath made her recoil.

She turned away, a feeling of dread seeping through her. Tears filled her eyes and she began to shiver. Outside she could hear the night patrol calling back and forth, enforcing the curfew.

Now what? she thought. There's no way we can buy our own railway tickets. Three children travelling alone would be questioned immediately. She shivered again. We'll have to be very, very careful, she thought. Someone might report us.

Elsbeth felt a slight stirring of guilt. This was her father's old friend. She should be sad and concerned for him. But try as she might, she could feel nothing for him. Just fear for herself and Emil.

Jaroslav was slouching against the far wall of the

bedroom. Elsbeth could hear him swearing softly in Czech. "What are we going to do now? This guy's dying."

"What do you mean, dying?" Elsbeth tore across the room. Half crying, half yelling, she pounded her fists against Jaroslav's chest. "Everyone said *we'd* die in that camp! But we didn't. And he's not going to die! You, me and Emil, we're going to make him better."

Jaroslav cowered and tried to push her away. "Okay, okay. Take it easy."

Elsbeth found herself swearing, but she did back off. Jaroslav has all these doubts all the time, she thought. He'll wear me down. We'll have more and more of these scenes and he'll drain me dry.

She felt the gnawing in her stomach and knew she needed food. I wish we'd saved more of the apples, she thought. Now, whatever we get has to be fed to Uncle Moritz. Abruptly she turned to Emil, who'd been watching the two of them wide-eyed.

"Emil, you keep an eye on Uncle Moritz. I'm going to look for some clean sheets. Jaroslav, go next door. Maybe that woman has some broth. Tell her we're here to look after him and she might even give us some cheese."

"I'm scared to be here alone with Uncle Moritz. I want to go to sleep." Emil was backing out of the room.

Elsbeth took a deep breath. "I won't be a second getting the sheets. I need your help, *liebchen*. You want to see Papa, don't you?" Elsbeth knew she was beginning to wheedle and hated herself for it. "I'll put you to bed in half an hour, I promise. Uncle Moritz has books downstairs. Some of them are in German. I'll read you a story, just like Papa used to. But right now, hold the candle and keep an eye on him. Please."

"A story?" Tentatively, Emil approached. "All right, then." He held the candle high and sat as far away from Uncle Moritz as he could, crinkling his nose. The mattress creaked as he swung his legs.

Elsbeth ran to the huge oak wardrobe standing in the hall. In the flickering light, she pulled out drawer after drawer until she found two worn linen sheets and some pillowcases. Grabbing them, she strode back to the bed. Uncle Moritz's chest rattled as he tried to breathe.

"Come on, Emil. You take the other side. I'll strip the dirty sheet off and put the fresh one down. Roll him over on his side towards you."

Jaroslav returned as the two of them were in the middle of the job. "Whew! He smells."

"Oh, shut up. I know the only reason we're getting him better is so he can help us, but how would you feel if it was you lying there helpless? Now get some magazines to put under his behind. We've got to protect these sheets till we can wash the others. Did you get any food?"

"That old woman asks too many questions. But she's really glad she doesn't have to come in every day and check on the old man. She gave me a small bowl of soup. It's downstairs in the kitchen. She said she'd get us a little cheese for tomorrow. She looked kind of scared, but I don't think she'll say anything to the police."

Elsbeth brought water and washed Uncle Moritz. Then, when he was resting comfortably, she arched her back and stretched. Emil started making shadow puppets against the wall in the candlelight. Elsbeth looked down at the old man, and a feeling of dread reached into her heart. She knew if she didn't sleep soon, she'd get sick.

"If Uncle Moritz dies, that nosy old woman is sure to find out. Then the police will be here in two seconds. Anyway, we've got to make him well. He can't die. He just can't. We've got to make *sure* he doesn't die."

"Are you crazy?" Jaroslav frowned. "How are we going to do that? He looks ready to croak right now."

"We need a routine, like we had in the camp. You slept earlier, so now it's my turn. Heat the broth and try to hold his head up so he'll drink some. If we make ourselves useful, he won't mind helping us out when he gets better."

"He could get arrested. He might not help us."

"He's our only chance and you know it." Elsbeth was exasperated with Jaroslav. "Tomorrow, I'm going to get Pater Wenzel to come and see Uncle Moritz. They went to school together before the Pater became a priest. While I'm gone you and Emil can start cleaning the house." She yawned and took Emil by the hand, drawing him out into the hall.

"Tonight, little brother, we're going to sleep under an eiderdown. Come on."

The first fingers of light were creeping along the alleys of Kaarlsbaad when Elsbeth woke with a start. She was so hungry she ached. The meat she'd eaten yesterday must have triggered these pains.

She lay restlessly, clenching her teeth, but finally slipped out of the carved oak bed to get a drink of water. Emil lay like a tousled teddy bear with only his head showing. He gave a small sigh and rolled over, still sleeping. She knew that the safety they were both feeling for the first time since their imprisonment was false.

Tiptoeing down the hall, she glanced into Uncle Moritz's bedroom, expecting to see Jaroslav reading. She couldn't believe her eyes. He lay snoring slightly, rolled up in a blanket on the floor.

Furious, Elsbeth clumped over to the bed. The bowl was empty. At least that fool had given Uncle Moritz some food. She bent over to put her ear close to the man's mouth. Years later, it seemed, she heard the dry, gasping breaths. She picked up his hand and felt for the pulse. Yes, there it was, faint but alive.

"What? What's wrong?" Jaroslav raised himself up, rubbing his shoulder where she had thumped him.

"Why didn't you stay awake? What if he'd stopped breathing? You were supposed to prop him up!" Elsbeth's face was flushed with anger and she turned her back to stand at the tiny window. The first tip of the sun was visible beyond the roofs of the town. "You're useless. If I want anything done, I have to do it myself." Her stomach grumbled as she spoke.

"How come you can sleep anyway? You must be as hungry as I am. The most I could sleep was four hours and here you are, out like a light. How come?"

"I don't know," Jaroslav mumbled as he got up. His hands seemed to fumble under his blanket.

Elsbeth went to get some water. She drank some, then remembering that old people get dehydrated very quickly, brought some back to Uncle Moritz.

"Wait a minute! Let me help you. Unless he's partly sitting up, the water could go into his lungs." Jaroslav lifted the man up, and to their surprise, he swallowed some water.

"Did you see that, Jaroslav?" Elsbeth almost shrieked as Uncle Moritz's eyes flew open, stared at her and then closed again. "We'll be in Eger sooner than we thought. Right now, you go to that woman and get some cheese." At the mention of food, a sharp pain clenched at her stomach and she bit her lip. "I'm going to get Pater Wenzel. In another half hour, he'll be saying seven o'clock Mass."

Jaroslav had bent over and was folding his blanket. Watching him, Elsbeth was grateful that he hadn't complained about being hungry. He isn't used to it the way Emil and I are, she thought.

On impulse, she paused on her way to the door and patted him on the back. As she did so, her toe kicked something under the blanket. Out rolled two apples.

"You have food!" She snatched the fruit. "You've been holding back. You knew how hungry

Emil and I were. We shared everything with you. How could you! I was right. You can't be trusted."

Elsbeth tore out the door and down the hall. She tucked the apples in beside Emil.

Down the stairs she ran, her anger pushing her out onto the street and halfway to the rectory. Ten minutes later, she slowed down. Suddenly afraid, she tried to walk sedately, the way she imagined a devout person going to early mass would walk.

If I'm challenged without Jaroslav here to do the talking, I'll be arrested, she thought. Trying to still the beating of her heart, she sniffed the faint aroma of ersatz coffee made from chicory and corn that some early riser had boiled. Her stomach constricted painfully and she wished she'd eaten one of the apples instead of leaving both for Emil.

"Yes? What do you want?" The old crone that kept house for Pater Wenzel had opened the heavy door of the rectory almost as soon as Elsbeth tugged the bell-pull.

Elsbeth smiled and pushed her way inside. "Pater Wenzel?"

Grumbling, the wizened old woman hobbled away. Did she notice my Austrian accent? Elsbeth wondered. At her age she probably didn't hear a word anyway . . .

"Yes?" The priest had emerged so quietly from the dark hallway that Elsbeth jumped.

"It's me, Elsbeth Hoffer." The priest frowned. "Don't you know me? I'm thinner and I'm older, but you must remember me."

"My child. When did you last eat? Of course I

remember you." The priest drew her towards the kitchen, and Elsbeth knew he hadn't recognized her. "We'll have some coffee, you and me, and we'll split an egg. Yes?"

Almost fainting at the thought of an egg, Elsbeth padded over the tile floor to the huge kitchen.

"I haven't seen Moritz, I've been so busy," Pater Wenzel sighed after Elsbeth had told him the story. "I didn't know he's so ill."

"We're worried about him. I know a visit from you would make him feel better."

"Yes. Yes. I'll come later. Maybe I could take him for a walk now and again when he's feeling better." The priest filled her cup again with the steaming liquid. Elsbeth felt almost stuffed and a bit sleepy.

"Could you play some cards with him? My father told me Uncle Moritz loves cards."

"How noble of you, my child, to take on such an endeavour. Just having children around the house again will make Moritz better." He frowned and turned away. "My thoughts are often with your father, but I cannot get involved. I cannot ask how he is. Or even where he is."

Elsbeth nodded and kept her fingers crossed under the table. She didn't dare tell even Pater Wenzel how desperate they were to make Uncle Moritz better. No one else could buy the train tickets to get them to Eger.

"I have to get back. Emil was sleeping when I left. Can we expect you soon, Pater?"

"I'll come for a few moments after Mass. I'll

bring your brother a piece of bread when I come. I guess I'll hardly know him either. This cursed war!"

"We have a Czech friend with us, Pater. Jaroslav is his name."

The priest looked surprised but said nothing as he gently closed the door behind her. Elsbeth knew he suspected something, but she trusted him. He couldn't help, but he wouldn't report them. She stepped briskly on the rough cobblestones. She didn't want to be caught out on the streets now that the townsfolk, including the police, would be going to work.

Over the next two weeks, with a bit of food several times a day and a clean house, Uncle Moritz began to sit up. He even got out of bed and went to the bathroom himself. Whispering in her ear, he told Elsbeth where he had some beets and potatoes hidden in the basement.

Every day Elsbeth heated a big pot of water on the stove, then poured it into a metal tub. There was no soap, so Emil just splashed around in it for a while. Then Elsbeth soaked in it. Finally Jaroslav took his turn.

"It's like a game," she said to Emil with a laugh.

"You don't smell like you used to," Emil said, laughing too.

How good it was to be in a home again! Elsbeth felt happiness creep into her heart like a long lost friend — but she still watched Jaroslav like a hawk, especially when it was his turn to do the cooking.

"Look, I didn't mean to hide those apples," he had tried to explain. "I didn't want to get weak."

"What about Emil and me?" Elsbeth had retorted. "I suppose you would have let us drop dead from starvation!"

One beautiful crisp day, Elsbeth decided to air Uncle Moritz's bedroom and change the linen. Downstairs, Pater Wenzel and her father's friend were playing cards. Elsbeth threw open the casement and drew back out of sight almost immediately.

"They're his relatives, they are." The voice of the woman next door floated upwards from the alleyway. "Very good they've come too. Ready for burial the old man was. Take it from me, that girl takes better care of him than his wife, God rest her soul, ever did."

"Where did they come from? What's their home town? Do you know their names?" The stranger's voice was deep and persistent. Elsbeth nearly fainted when she peeked down and saw the brown uniform of the Kaarlsbaad police. Somebody must have reported us, she thought. They'll go on asking questions and then they'll come in.

"Hey! Shut the window! It's too cold!"

"Shut up, Jaroslav," Elsbeth hissed as she quietly closed the window. "We've got to get out of here. The police are next door. We can't wait for Uncle Moritz to get better. He's taking too long."

Slowly she walked to the bed and sat down. A terrible numbness seemed to paralyze her. She waited for the knock at Uncle Moritz's door. But the minutes ticked by and no knock came. Just asking questions today, she thought.

"We can't get out of here without your Uncle Moritz. There's no way they'll sell train tickets to three kids." Jaroslav paced back and forth. "I'm going home. It's better than staying with you two and getting arrested with you."

"You can't leave us. We need you. How can we get over the border if we can't speak Czech?" Elsbeth's face was white with panic. She knew she had to persuade Jaroslav to stay with them.

"You'll get your father shot if you go back," she continued. "They'll know he sent you with us. You said so yourself."

"You're trying to frighten me into staying."

"Go back if you want to." Elsbeth jumped up and ran to the window. "I'll call the police right now. You can watch them drag Emil and me off. They won't do anything to you here in Kaarlsbaad, but wait till you get back to Saaz." Elsbeth struggled with the lock on the casement, praying he wouldn't let her go through with her bluff.

"No. Don't open it. I'll stay."

Elsbeth's knees buckled. Weak with relief, she collapsed into Aunt Irmtraud's rocking chair. As Jaroslav continued to pace, she closed her eyes. Perhaps it was the chair, for suddenly the image of her white-haired honorary aunt was very strong. Elsbeth remembered watching her make her way through the streets before the war. The memory somehow comforted her and she relaxed. Aunt Irmtraud had died three years ago, but all her clothes were still hanging in the closets . . .

Abruptly Elsbeth jumped up. "I've got it, Jaroslav! *I'll* buy the train tickets."

"Yeah, sure. Or I'll do it. Or get Emil to do it." Jaroslav slumped down on the bed. "We're finished. We might as well give up."

"No." Elsbeth was almost chortling. "We'll be in Bayreuth and with Papa by next week." She got up and went over to sit beside him. "Listen, this is what we're going to do." She leaned towards him and outlined her plan.

"It might work." Jaroslav frowned. "The main problem we have is Emil. He's got to keep his mouth shut in the station *and* on the train." He hesitated. "It's risky."

"Would you rather go back to Saaz and watch your father get shot?"

"No. But what about Uncle Moritz? Will he report that we're gone?"

"He saw lots of people on the run during the war. We helped him. I know he's grateful. The danger's not from Uncle Moritz."

After lunch, when Uncle Moritz was napping, Elsbeth tied a pillow across her back with Jaroslav's help. She took a shovelful of ashes from the tile fireplace in the kitchen and rubbed them into her hair. From the basement she took a few heads of garlic and tied them together to wear around her neck. Then she pulled one of Aunt Irmtraud's printed dresses on over her head and pinned the cord of her gold pince-nez spectacles to the collar. Jaroslav rubbed some ashes under her eyes and on her face so it appeared lined.

Elsbeth popped a garlic bud into her mouth and chewed it as she tied a babushka over her hair.

"Phew! You smell." Jaroslav backed away. "Why are you chewing the garlic?"

Emil jumped to her defence as he smeared some more ashes onto her hands. "My sister's the smartest person in the whole word."

"It'll keep everyone at a distance." She opened a cupboard. "I wish we could make up a mustard plaster too." She walked out to the front hall and picked up her aunt's carved walking cane.

"Let's go. Remember, you two, I'm too deaf to speak. Jaroslav will do all the talking as usual. Emil, if you ever want to see Papa again, then *don't say one word* down at the railway station."

She opened the front door and stepped out onto the street, an elderly and stooped old grandmother, followed by her two grandchildren.

"Next stop Eger," she whispered.

"Then Bayreuth and Papa!" Emil gave a couple of skips.

"Shut up, Emil. Not one more word."

6

Next Stop Eger

*E*lsbeth muttered to herself as the three of them entered the cavernous Kaarlsbaad railway station. She made her hands shake a little and coughed every now and then. She was very frightened. She kept Emil's wet palm in a viselike grip and was grateful to see the look of terror on his face as they wound their way to the ticket counter. His lips were sealed, all right.

The ticket seller gave the three of them a quick glance. He asked some questions in Czech as he punched out three passes.

Jaroslav answered him. Then he grinned and jerked his head towards Elsbeth, and said something else in a lower voice.

The man laughed.

Can we trust Jaroslav? Elsbeth wondered. He's too jaunty, and I don't understand what he's saying. "Eh, eh?" she squeaked, cupping her hand around her ear. She was afraid Jaroslav might be giving her away.

But no, the man held out the tickets.

Jaroslav took Elsbeth's elbow as she waddled across the huge station.

"What was that all about?" she hissed. "What did you tell him?"

"It's all right. He asked why we were taking Grandmother to Eger. I said to visit Grandpa's grave and then to stay awhile with my aunt. I said the way Grandma smells, we'll have a compartment to ourselves."

Elsbeth couldn't help but smile. Suddenly, though, her heart was in her mouth. The biggest test lay right ahead. If they could get their tickets punched and get onto the platform, they would be home free.

"What if the conductor challenges us?" Jaroslav whispered.

"Just shut up and pray that he doesn't," Elsbeth whispered. "You were smart-alecky enough back there to get us thrown in jail."

As they walked up the ramp, Elsbeth held her breath and kept her head down.

"The old mother's sick, is she?" The conductor leaned back from them as he punched their tickets. Jaroslav nodded, and the conductor was about to wave them through when he frowned and stared hard at Elsbeth. He started to say something, but the sound of drunken singing distracted him. A man staggered up the ramp, crashing into the people waiting behind Elsbeth and then into her.

"Whew! What's *she* been drinking?" he lisped, breathing out schnapps all over everybody.

"Go on through. Go on through." The conductor waved them on as he tried to keep the drunk from falling on him.

Once they were safely on the platform, Jaroslav hustled them to the other side of an empty little kiosk, once overflowing with sandwiches and newspapers. They sat on a bench and, as casually as they could, pretended to be reading the books they had "borrowed" from Uncle Moritz. We just have to look as if we are locals, Elsbeth had warned them.

A young man sidled towards them and flattened himself against the kiosk, out of sight of the ramp leading from the station.

Someone yelled and Elsbeth looked up. Hands shaking, she took up her glasses and fastened them on her nose as feet pounded along the platform.

Suddenly the young man made a break for it. In less than a minute three men in frayed uniforms had dragged him down and were beating him about the head with nightsticks.

Elsbeth reached for Emil and pulled his face to her shoulder so he wouldn't see. They had both watched similar scenes many times before. But Jaroslav had never come face to face with someone accused of being a political enemy. Or the consequences.

The young man's screams bruised this woman, tore at that man, ripped between all the ticket holders as they tried to sit or stand still, waiting for the train, praying that they would be invisible.

Jaroslav moaned and covered his ears with his hands. Finally he jumped up and started towards the fracas.

"Sit down, you fool," hissed Elsbeth. "Do you want to be beaten up like him?"

Pale and angry, Jaroslav hesitated, then collapsed beside her just as the puffing of the ancient steam engine sounded from down the track. Amid all the hissing and yelling that drowned out the beating, the train stopped at the long platform.

"You were lucky they didn't see you. Pull yourself together."

At the conductor's cry, they all boarded. No one questioned an arthritic grandmother, bent over and smelly, so pale, with one grandchild clinging to her and another leading the way along the corridor.

Huddled over, Elsbeth followed Jaroslav. She was relieved that this was an express train and that it wasn't crowded.

"Give me a hand, Emil. The door's stuck." Jaroslav tugged and pushed at the door of the compartment while Elsbeth, hunched over Aunt Irmtraud's cane, waited. All their belongings, including two cooked potatoes, were in a big wicker basket strapped on her back. One of the other passengers, attempting to squeeze past them, made a rude remark. Elsbeth bent lower and coughed as if she hadn't heard.

Suddenly the handle twisted and the door swung inward. An elderly man stood smiling, holding it for them to enter — until he got a whiff of Elsbeth.

Then he stumbled back, crossing himself and muttering in Czech.

Probably afraid I have the plague or something, Elsbeth thought. She gave a cackle and continued stomping down the passageway. "Find an empty one down at the end," she whispered to Jaroslav, who pushed past her. He looked through the glass into each compartment, but they were all occupied.

"You stink." Emil was scuffing his shoes as he trailed along behind Elsbeth.

She whirled around. "Don't say one word. Not one." She felt like shaking him. "Remember Mama? I'll be dragged off just like her if anyone hears you speaking German. They'll drag you off too. So *keep quiet.*"

Emil's lower lip started to tremble, but Elsbeth refused to weaken. To save both of them, she had to be mean to him now. Jaroslav beckoned from the end and she shuffled towards him. He had found one empty compartment. Three hours, she thought as she sat down, and we'll be in Eger. I hope the potatoes will be enough to get us across the mountains to the border.

Elsbeth stared at Jaroslav's reflection shaking in the window glass. Could he have more food hidden in his pockets? she wondered. We'll see. She watched as he brought out an ancient pocket checkers set and began to play a game with Emil.

The swaying of the train soothed her. It seemed to be saying "Papa, Papa" over and over as it carried them east. She looked out the window for a while, but finally leaned her head back to sleep.

We should stop only a couple of times, she thought as she drifted off, for mail or water.

"Good day." Elsbeth's eyes flew open as the door banged against the seat. The noise and dust from the corridor had swept a bearded stranger into their midst.

Elsbeth felt confused and struggled to keep her wits about her as the stranger stared down at her. She hunched down and shifted closer to Emil.

"Good day," Jaroslav replied in Czech. Then in response to the man's question, he said, "Eger."

Elsbeth popped another clove of garlic in her mouth and chewed, making loud noises.

The man continued talking to Jaroslav and suddenly turned and addressed Elsbeth.

"Eh? Eh?" Elsbeth cupped her hand around her ear. Emil opened his mouth to speak, but Elsbeth squeezed him so hard he kept quiet, looking guilty. The man shrugged, then took out an old magazine and began to read.

Elsbeth was terrified. She felt sick. Emil's sure to start babbling, she thought, her mouth as dry as the desert. How much farther to Eger? she wondered.

As if in answer, the man looked at his watch and said, "Half an hour more." That Elsbeth understood. She could almost feel Papa's arms around her, as her heart lurched.

She sat, counting the minutes, until Emil, bored, wriggled out from her clasp and lowered the window to hang outside. Suddenly he gave a whoop. "Eger!" he shouted.

Before he could say one more word, Jaroslav was beside him, his hand digging hard into the boy's shoulder. They both laughed and pointed at the faint outline of buildings in the distance. The stranger cupped his hands to light a black-market cigarette. But Elsbeth knew he hadn't missed a trick. He'd been watching the three of them closely.

Without warning the train slowed and shuddered to a stop. People were running and yelling outside. The stranger stepped to the window and looked out. Then he spoke to Jaroslav.

Jaroslav replied, and the man opened the door and jumped out onto the grass. He walked up towards the front where the engine had stopped under a water tower.

"What did he say?" Elsbeth tugged at Jaroslav who was staring after the man.

"The valve switch in the control is broken. The train can't move until it's fixed. His father drove trains, so he went to help."

"Eger's right there, so close we can almost touch it." The frustration Elsbeth felt showed in every word she spoke.

"He said we should stay on the train until we get right into Eger."

"Why? Why would he say something like that?" All Elsbeth's fear came tumbling back.

"I don't know." Jaroslav sat down again.

"I want a drink of water." Emil wrenched loose from Jaroslav, jumped down onto the grass and began running towards the tower.

Mouths gaping, Elsbeth and Jaroslav watched as he caught up with the bearded stranger and slipped a hand into his. The stranger smiled down at him, and to their astonishment took an enamel cup out of his rucksack, filled it from a tap nearby and handed it to Emil.

Elsbeth couldn't watch any more. She slumped down on the seat as a tear welled up and rolled down her cheek.

"He drank the first one, now he's bringing us some." There was a glint of admiration in Jaroslav's voice.

"That man is nice," Emil said when he'd hopped back into the compartment. "He gave me this for you." He held the cup out to Elsbeth.

"That man could send us back to the camp, don't you understand?" She slammed the cup out of Emil's hand.

"That was stupid. We're both thirsty." Jaroslav kicked at the cup and it rolled under the seat.

"You'll know what thirst is when we all get sent back to Saaz." Like a cannonball, Elsbeth was pounding at Jaroslav's chest, crying and hiccupping. "We were almost free! *Free*." She threw herself onto the seat, and pummelling the leather, she sobbed and sobbed. Outside the yelling and banging continued, drowning out the sounds of her weeping.

She fought to regain control of herself, calling upon all her strength to choke back her sobbing. As she struggled, she became aware that the compartment was ominously silent. She raised herself on one elbow to see the stranger standing silently, watching her.

Jaroslav was staring at her, stunned. The stranger and Emil eyed each other. Elsbeth's babushka had slipped off, and the ash ran in rivulets down her cheeks, making her younger by the minute.

Chuckling, the stranger leaned over and patted Elsbeth on the shoulder. "You are brave children," he said in mangled German. Digging into his rucksack, he brought out an enormous salami and cut off big pieces for each of them. Then, still smiling, he put his finger to his lips in the gesture of silence. Elsbeth finally regained her dignity by sitting up very straight. But she felt exhausted as she took bites of the meat.

"Thank you," Jaroslav muttered as he dug in.

"You have been clever. That should be rewarded, not punished." The man smiled and cut off yet another chunk of meat for each of them.

Slowly the pistons began to roll again and the train chugged towards Eger. With each swallow, Elsbeth felt more and more hysterical. She began to giggle, then couldn't stop. Jaroslav and Emil joined in, and soon everyone was laughing, including the stranger. We're going to make it after all, Elsbeth thought. No one can stop us now.

But after fifteen minutes, the train slowed down again. It stopped at a depot on the outskirts of Eger. The stranger frowned and stepped to the window to see what was happening this time.

"Police," he said to Jaroslav, who translated.

"They're searching every compartment. Something about a missing boy."

"*Come on.*" Elsbeth pulled off Aunt Irmtraud's dress and yanked off the pillow. Standing tall at last, she opened the door into the passageway. "We'll have to jump off the train. We can get away across the tracks on the other side."

Jaroslav hung back. "The trains come from all directions all the time. We could get hit."

"It's dangerous, but it's the only way we'll get out of here. Come on, Emil. Hang on tight to me. Do whatever I do!"

The stranger's blessing, "God go with you," hung on the air as they hurried to the end of the corridor and jumped from the train.

7

Into the Mountains

Crouching low, trying not to panic, Elsbeth, Emil and Jaroslav stumbled across the maze of tracks that led into and out of Eger. Peeking back, Elsbeth could look under the train and see the leather boots of the police.

"We've got to be out of sight by the time the police are finished," she called back to Jaroslav. Lights were flashing and bells clanging as trains shunted back and forth. The three of them hopped across this set of tracks, and scurried behind that shunting train, aiming for the road at the far side and the field beyond it.

"Train! Get down." Jaroslav shoved Elsbeth to the ground. As she fell, she grabbed for Emil, wrapping her hand like a lash around his wrist. She heard a faint thud as Jaroslav's body hit the wooden ties behind her.

"Get *down*, Emil! Lie as flat as you can!" Elsbeth

threw herself down and pushed Emil's head into the dirt on the bed between the tracks. He yelled and struggled for a second, then the roar of the steam engine behind them drowned out every sound. The engineer kept blowing the whistle over and over, but the train was going too fast to stop.

"Keep your head down or you'll lose it! Keep your behind down too!" Screaming uselessly, Elsbeth pulled in her own stomach and spread out like a wounded bird.

The huge black steam engine deafened them as it raced overhead. A solid wall of sound pressed Elsbeth's face into the cinders so hard it drew blood. Freight car after freight car rolled over them. The temptation to raise her head, to struggle up, was overwhelming. This was the only time in her life she was glad they'd been starved in the camp. Their thin bodies left space to spare.

Terrified, Elsbeth was hardly aware of the fresh air brushing against her hair. The last car had rumbled over her, and her body lay beneath the dusk of bright evening. Still flattened against the ties, her hand pressing Emil's head down, she twisted around to see if another train was coming. But all she saw was Jaroslav getting to his knees very slowly.

"You saved our lives," she gasped. She couldn't believe what he'd done. "Are you all right, Emil?"

Elsbeth's whole body was shaking so much she could hardly struggle to her feet. Emil's breath was coming in great sobs and his legs seemed to be made of rubber as he tried to stand up.

"It's all right, *liebchen*. It's all right." Elsbeth helped Emil to his feet and brushed him off, kissing both his cheeks. Emil threw his arms around her and clung so tightly it almost took her breath away. White-faced, she lifted her head towards the highlands that rose beyond the out-skirts of Eger. They're not too high and not too steep, she thought, struggling to revive from the numbing shock.

"I'm scared, Elsbeth."

"We'll make it yet, Emil." As she turned to Jaroslav, she saw him sway slightly. His face looked almost green. "Come on, we've got to go."

Crouching low again, they moved, stumbling at first, and then, as their strength returned, running, until they reached the road and crossed it.

"That was close." Jaroslav threw himself down in the tall grass, licking the blood from his lip where he'd bitten right through it.

"We've got to get out of here." Elsbeth's voice sounded hollow even to herself. "There's a path over there, leading into the mountains."

"How far's the border?" Jaroslav was wiping his lip.

"About ten kilometres, your father said." Elsbeth hugged Emil as she pulled him from where he'd curled himself up like a baby.

"That's easy."

"That's as the crow flies. It'll be a lot farther than that for us." She scanned a red sky full of clouds that looked like sheep skittering across the brisk September horizon. A shiver ran through her.

"We've got to find a way to survive tonight. It'll be so cold in the mountains."

"What about patrols?" Jaroslav shivered too.

"I want Papa."

"Hush, Emil." Elsbeth wiped his face gently and put her arm around his shoulders as they started off. "We'll see Papa soon. The day after tomorrow. Then we'll go across a huge ocean to Canada."

"What's Canada?" Emil wiped his nose on his sleeve and looked a little happier.

"It's a great big country. Bigger than all of Europe. It's full of Eskimos and polar bears and they have lots of snow."

"There's more Indians in Canada than Eskimos," Jaroslav called out from behind.

"They might scalp us." Emil was almost crying again.

"Don't be silly Emil. That's only in stories."

Jaroslav caught up to them. "I saw a picture of a War Dance once. Only the men danced. They wore feather headdresses and danced to drums. It looked like fun."

"I don't want to live in Canada. I want Mama." Emil grabbed Elsbeth again.

"You're just tired, little Emil." Elsbeth hugged him. "Canada is free. *Free*. No camps. No police checks on every corner for passports." Then, looking aside, she added in a low voice, "Mama's gone. We both know that."

Almost at the foothills, Jaroslav hesitated. "We've got to watch out for others trying to sneak across. And what about the patrols?"

"Every half hour, I think. I'm not sure. Now, no more talking. Do you hear, Emil? Just whispering from now on. We don't want to be sent back with Papa waiting, do we?"

"You and Emil can use my belt." Jaroslav held out the buckle to Elsbeth, while Emil took hold of the end. "Hang onto it and we won't get lost when we leave the path. Or when it gets dark. I'll bring up the rear."

"I hope there's a moon so we can see to go around the villages."

"What if there's another boar?" Emil was looking nervously around.

"Soldiers come here all the time. Any boar would have been eaten by now."

Elsbeth turned to them and put her finger to her lips as they began to climb parallel to the path. There must be one patrol ahead of us and one behind, she thought. How can we time them?

As it grew darker, Elsbeth realized that the moonlight wouldn't penetrate the forest. The only light came from the searchlight that swept the sky overhead. The silence seemed almost threatening as they climbed on.

A sudden loud *crack* made them all jump.

"A rifle shot," hissed Jaroslav.

"*Run!*" Elsbeth dropped the belt and grabbed Emil by the hand, scrambling up onto a sandstone outcropping that jutted over the embankment and the path. "Come on," she said in a low voice. "We can hide up here." She threw herself flat, dragging Emil down beside her.

Jaroslav's footsteps scuffled right behind her, and she heard the dull thud as he fell down beside them.

They lay on the carpet of dried needles, holding their breath. But there were no running feet or yelling patrols. Nothing happened. There was just a terrible stillness. They waited.

"Maybe a deer stepped on a branch," Elsbeth whispered at last, as she began to breathe again.

"We should time the patrols," Jaroslav whispered back.

"But how can we? We haven't a watch." Just the mention of patrols made Elsbeth's mouth dry.

Jaroslav cupped his hand over Elsbeth's ear so she could hear him. "We'll watch the first one go by, and then count the number of sweeps from the searchlight until the next one comes."

They lay so still that they might have been three branches fallen on the ground. They strained their eyes against the darkness, but could see nothing. Elsbeth began to shiver against the dampness. She was raising herself on one elbow when she heard a soft new sound, not far away. Jaroslav pulled on her arm. She dropped down again and pressed Emil even flatter.

Like ghosts drifting out of the fog, two men in uniform seemed to float by slowly a little distance below them on the path. They carried rifles and walked one behind the other. Emil gave a tiny squeak and burrowed his face even deeper into the pine needles. But the soldiers kept on going. It seemed years before Elsbeth relaxed, knowing they were safe.

"Now we'll count the searchlight sweeps in the sky till the next patrol." Jaroslav had raised his head and was keeping track with his fingers.

They lay, trying not to think about the cold, waiting silently. Elsbeth thought her hands would drop off, they were so icy. Then, once again, a quiet footstep sounded. For the second time, two men passed below them, one behind and one in front. Again, Elsbeth's heart almost stopped.

Finally, the soldiers gone, they sat up.

"I counted sixty sweeps of the searchlight." Jaroslav was rubbing his legs and arms trying to get warm.

"There's a cave here." Emil's loud whisper pierced the darkness and then became fainter as he crawled inside.

"Wait for us." Elsbeth and Jaroslav crawled after him. Just inside the black opening they hesitated, but the three of them instinctively felt the cave was empty. They stumbled against rock and wall — and tripped over something rough.

They froze. Emil bent down and fingered what lay beneath their feet. "It feels like a coat," he whispered, picking it up. They took it to the mouth of the cave where they could see a little better.

"Feel these buttons. Maybe it was from a Russian officer." Jaroslav began going through the pockets.

"It might have been a partisan." Emil's whisper sounded squeaky. "Maybe somebody working for Czechoslovakia."

"Ouch." Jaroslav sucked on his finger. "Something bit me."

"These buttons have wings on them. Maybe it was a Canadian pilot who bailed out after a raid and had to hide. Anyway, somebody waited in here for the war to end."

Jaroslav felt his way along the wall, towards the back. Elsbeth and Emil heard him fumbling. "I found some branches," he whispered. "Maybe I can make a fire by rubbing two together."

"What a stupid idea! We're dead if you do." Elsbeth found herself almost shrieking.

"But I'm cold."

"We've got the coat."

"The coat's probably crawling with lice." Jaroslav had grabbed it and was holding it between thumb and forefinger far away from himself.

"*We* were crawling with lice until we got to Uncle Moritz's." First he helps us, then he does something dumb, Elsbeth thought. She didn't know what to make of Jaroslav. She knew only that her stomach hurt and she had to eat soon. "It would take us at least an hour to get a big enough pile of pine needles to sleep on. This coat is a blessing."

Elsbeth's knees gave out and she slid down against the rock wall. Emil snuggled up beside her. Jaroslav shrugged and collapsed beside Emil. He made a point of covering Elsbeth and Emil with most of the coat, saving only a corner for himself. Within minutes he began to scratch and say "Ouch."

"We'd better eat the potatoes now, so we can

sleep. It's the last of our food." Carefully, Elsbeth broke the precious tubers into pieces for each of them. Once, she had hated potatoes, but now she had to hold herself back from gulping them down. Her stomach hurt even more once she began to swallow. "It *is* the last of the food, isn't it, Jaroslav?"

But Jaroslav, having downed his portion, had rolled over on his side and didn't answer her. At least if he tries to eat something, we'll see him, Elsbeth thought, closing her eyes.

That night, her dreams drifted back to before the war. She remembered Uncle Fred arriving for Christmas carrying a struggling carp. They'd raced upstairs and put it in the bathtub. It swam around until Christmas Eve when all the aunts, uncles and cousins came to share it.

She dreamed she was walking to school, carrying her English, Latin and mathematics books. She kept waving and joking with her girlfriends. Then suddenly there was rifle fire and two of them dropped, blood all over them. Pain made her cry in her sleep until the face of her Latin teacher, Professor Brauthofen, swam in front of her. He was quoting his favourite saying, "*Aut inveniam viam aut faciam.*" I'll find a way, or make one.

Slowly all the pain drained out of her, and she slept.

8

No Man's Land

As they climbed higher and higher the next day, nibbling at a few stray berries close to the path and drinking from mountain streams, Elsbeth wondered if she'd misjudged Jaroslav. He saved my life, she thought. But in the back of her heart she still didn't trust him.

Elsbeth found herself getting irritable as the day progressed. She was very hungry. They sighted a small village clinging to the side of the mountain, but, of course, they had to go around it. Elsbeth heard a rooster crowing. She resented not being able to beg for an egg. Emil, trudging along beside her, became quieter and quieter. Elsbeth wondered if he was sick.

"There it is! There's Wunsiedel!" At last they had reached the top of the mountain and broken through the forest into a large clearing. They stood quietly, staring way down below. Wunsiedel was on the American side.

"There's No Man's Land." Jaroslav's hand was shaking as he pointed. "We've made it."

"We're not across yet." Elsbeth looked around nervously. "We could get shot, standing in the open like this." She could see the wide line of barren land below, cleared of all trees, flanked on both the Czech and the German side with barbed wire. "Look, Emil! See all that dust? Over there in Germany? That's an American jeep. Tonight we'll see Papa."

"Is Papa in Bayreuth?"

"I hope so. That's where he said to wait for him, anyway. Come on." Half sliding, half stumbling, Elsbeth skirted the edge of the forest as she started down the other side of the mountain. She could hear Emil and Jaroslav running behind her. She was about to enter the protection of the forest again when she tumbled head over heels, hitting her head. Jaroslav grabbed her by the arm and stopped her fall.

"What's wrong? You never stumbled before."

"What do you think's wrong? I'm hungry."

"All right, all right. You can have an apple." Jaroslav dug into the pocket of his jacket. "I kept two back."

"You're horrible," screamed Emil, hurling himself onto Jaroslav, punching and hitting him.

He's worse than anyone in the camp, Elsbeth thought. He doesn't even understand what he's done. There's no hope for him.

Jaroslav brushed Emil off as easily as if he were a moth. "You always had a family," he began, his voice tight with emotion as he stood panting in front of them. "You had each other. I had no one. My mother died when I was three. My father worked all the time. I hardly saw him. I look after myself. Just me."

"Anyway," he mumbled, holding out the fruit in his hand, "it's lucky I did hide these. We need our wits tonight to get across No Man's Land." To Elsbeth's surprise he gave both apples to her and Emil.

The wind whistling through the pines and the cry of the hawk circling overhead were the only sounds that broke the stillness. Elsbeth stared at Jaroslav. Was this an admission, at last, that he needed them? As she tasted the sweet juice and felt her energy revive, she found she didn't care. She knew only that once they were safe, she never wanted to see him again.

"Let's go, Elsbeth." Emil must have felt the same. Eating, he turned his back on Jaroslav and took his sister's hand. They descended silently towards the border.

Elsbeth kept looking over her shoulder. The patrols behind us must be closer than before, she thought. We wasted too much time arguing. But to her relief, she didn't see anyone.

Finally, a couple of hours later, their feet touched level ground. Elsbeth could hardly believe it. The apple she'd eaten had taken away her hunger and her heart beat madly, but, instead of joy, she felt empty inside. She stared through the evergreens at the barbed wire in the distance.

Suddenly she heard an alien sound. "Quick. Into that grove of trees," she hissed, pulling them aside. "I think I hear voices."

Lying flat, Elsbeth expected to see heavy boots and brown uniforms pass by. Instead, through the trees, which had thinned out this close to the border, she saw three civilians. Two men and a woman. They looked all around, then raced to the barbed wire. One man began cutting while the others kept watch.

"We should have brought wire cutters," Jaroslav muttered.

Finished, the man held the wire apart while the other man and the woman wrenched their way through. Then they held the wire for him. All three of them raced across No Man's Land for the other side.

"They made it." Elsbeth watched almost in disbelief.

Having reached the American side at the German border, the first man was cutting the wire when loud shouts from the Czech side made them look back. Elsbeth gasped. The man and woman feverishly shoved their way through to safety. A shot rang out. The man who'd held the wire for the others dropped and lay as still as a stone.

"Oh, no!" Emil's voice quivered. "We'll never get across, Elsbeth. There's too many patrols."

Two soldiers came out of the woods, far off to their right. Terrified, Elsbeth, Emil and Jaroslav clung to the ground and watched from their hiding place. Rapidly the soldiers repaired the hole in the fence and then vanished back into the woods. Elsbeth caught a flash of brown up on the path they'd come from.

"That guy got killed because there was nothing to distract those soldiers," Jaroslav whispered as they lay still, waiting to see if another patrol would appear.

"We've got to find better cover. How about that clump of low bushes over there?" Elsbeth began to crawl towards them. Jaroslav threw the coat over his shoulder and followed behind Emil.

"Good thing we brought the coat. It can keep us warm while we think up a diversion." Jaroslav spread out the coat and sat down on it. "Hey, what's this?" He raised himself and fumbled underneath in a hidden inside pocket to withdraw a small metal box. "Matches! We could have had a fire without any trouble at all."

He's so stupid, Elsbeth thought. He doesn't listen to anything I say. But she knew that Jaroslav was right about needing a diversion.

"How'll we get through the fence, Elsbeth?" Emil was shivering as he crawled close to her on the coat.

"We'll hold the wire up for each other. We can slip right under. We're so thin, we'll get through in a flash."

"Yeah. And we'll get what that guy got." Jaroslav sounded frightened.

"I'm not asking *you* to hold the wire up, Jaroslav. I'll do it. Emil and you can go through first. I don't care. I'm going to be in Bayreuth tomorrow no matter what."

But Elsbeth knew she had no idea how to create a diversion that would draw the patrols away from them. For the next half hour she and Jaroslav whispered, tossing ideas back and forth. Once they glimpsed yet another patrol in the distance.

A rising sense of panic began to dull Elsbeth's mind. She struggled to suppress it, but she knew none of their ideas would work.

Jaroslav groaned and stood up to stretch. "You were right. You know, back there in the cave. A fire would have drawn the patrols right to us."

Both their faces lit up at the same time. Elsbeth jumped to her feet and hugged him. "You've got it. Come on. The patrol just left. We can make a pile of pine needles back there, behind those trees, well out of sight of the patrols." She stuck her finger in her mouth, then held it up to see where the wind was coming from. "We'll set fire to it when we're ready to go. With this wind it'll blow back against the mountainside away from No Man's Land."

"Right." Jaroslav grinned at her. "Tonight we *will* be in Bayreuth."

For the next half hour the three of them worked feverishly. The ground was thick with dried-out needles and their pile grew rapidly.

"We've got to have time to get from the pile, back through the trees and then down to the fence without being seen." Elsbeth threw some dry branches onto the pile.

"Don't worry." Jaroslav built up the pile even more. "They'll be in a panic. They'll think the whole forest is going up in flames."

They ran in a crouch back to their hiding place and waited. "We'll go across just after sunset. The light plays tricks then and that'll help us." Elsbeth settled herself in to wait.

"Okay, they're gone." Jaroslav got up and stretched quickly. "It's zero hour. I'm going back now to light the fire. Then I'll join you back here." He hesitated, not able to meet Elsbeth's eyes. "You said you'd hold up the wire so Emil and I can get through."

Elsbeth felt such contempt well up in her that she could hardly speak. Everything he did for us, he did to save his own skin, she thought. He needed us to get himself out. Grudgingly she admitted that his warning yell on the tracks had saved her and Emil. But anybody would probably yell if a train was going to run over somebody.

"Wait till the fire's well caught," Elsbeth said coldly, drawing Emil close to her.

They waited and waited. Worried, Elsbeth was about to set off herself, when she saw Jaroslav running towards them.

"Let's go," he panted. "The first few matches wouldn't light. I had to find one that wasn't damp." Behind him, in the distance, flames were dancing up and spreading, catching small bushes and trees.

Elsbeth leaped up and grabbed Emil's hand. Together, they raced as fast as they could to the barbed wire fence. She lifted it up and shoved Emil under. Jaroslav wiggled through, then he and Emil held the wire up for her.

"Run, Emil!" Elsbeth yelled as she wriggled under the fence. She leaped up to race to the other side of No Man's Land clutching Emil's hand. She was lost in time and space, as her legs pounded. Jaroslav passed her and somehow she knew she'd dropped Emil's hand. Jaroslav will be the first to get to the other side, she thought.

"Elsbeth! My ankle!" Emil's scream stopped Elsbeth in her tracks. She turned. Emil was lying on the ground, his face twisted in pain.

Elsbeth glanced back at Jaroslav. He hesitated and then continued running towards freedom. She wheeled around and raced back to Emil. He had fallen only a third of the way across.

"I'll carry you," she panted, bending to help him up. She heard shouts and looked back towards Czechoslovakia. Flames were stretching towards the sky. A siren sounded.

"You can't. I'm too heavy." Emil was crying as he tried to push himself up on one foot. "I'll have to hop the rest of the way."

"You can't hop! It's too slow!" Elsbeth and Emil stared at one another, eyes filled with death.

Suddenly Elsbeth heard someone running and felt the ground shake a little. Not daring to believe, she half turned around. Jaroslav! He's coming back to help us! she thought, afraid he might vanish.

Jaroslav was running doubled over, grunting from the pain of a stitch in his side. His face was streaked with sweat when he finally reached them. "We'll carry Emil together," he panted. "I'll take his other arm."

"Thank you, Jaroslav," Elsbeth said, standing as straight as she could and looking directly at him. "We will not forget this." This is *his* miracle, she thought. He's risked his life to save us.

"Come on!" Jaroslav grumbled. "We'll get shot if you keep on talking."

Together, they gripped Emil under each armpit and lifted him well off the ground. Half stumbling, half running, they covered what seemed like a million kilometres.

Lungs on fire, staggering the last couple of steps, Elsbeth reached the wire. Grabbing it, she cried out in pain. A barb had punctured her skin. "*Get under, Emil.*"

Fast as an eel, her brother wiggled into the American zone. Jaroslav followed and held the wire up. Finally, almost sobbing, Elsbeth got through and struggled to her knees, and then to her feet. They were safe at last.

"*We're free!*" she yelled.

Whooping and staggering almost hysterically, Elsbeth and Jaroslav carried Emil towards the road.

"Halt! Halt or I'll shoot." The American soldier sprang out of nowhere between them and the road to Bayreuth. His rifle had snapped up to his shoulder ready to fire.

"Don't move!" Elsbeth panted in German. "He'll kill us."

They stood absolutely still. The American soldier circled around them. "Came alone, did you?" he muttered.

Frozen, Elsbeth watched as a jeep ground to a halt on the road beyond and the largest man she'd ever seen got out. "What's the problem, soldier?" he yelled to the guard.

"They've got to go back. I have my orders, sir." He thrust his rifle aggressively, motioning the three of them back towards Czechoslovakia. "All you people, always trying to get across the border all the time. None of you got any papers." He began crowding them, pushing them. "Go on. Back you go." Elsbeth struggled frantically to hold her ground as the big man approached. Emil was groaning as he knelt in the grass.

Elsbeth dropped beside Emil and clung to him. "Papers?" she blurted out in halting English. "Wait! Wait! We have papers." She reached clumsy fingers inside her sweater and unpinned the papers Herr Jindrich had given them a thousand years ago. Hand shaking, she held them out. "Good. Papers good. We not go back. *Never!*"

Startled, the soldier stepped back as she jumped up and spread her arms wide. "Shoot us. Shoot us," she could hear herself pleading. "We never go back."

"Easy, miss. Take it easy." Wide-eyed, Elsbeth watched the huge man hold out his hand. "Are their papers in order, soldier?"

Loud honking interrupted them. Another jeep had arrived and parked up on the road behind the first one. A nurse jumped out while another one stood up and yelled. "What about that extra help you promised me? We're going crazy over at the hospital. Remember?"

"Hang on a second, will you?" the sergeant called over his shoulder. "*Are* their papers in order, soldier?"

"Yeah. Yeah. Every bunch that comes across has papers in order, sir. But we got orders to send them back. I'll get busted if I don't."

"Kids. They're just kids. And the young one looks hurt." The sergeant's voice was low. "We can't send them back. Their papers are in order, right?"

The soldier nodded as the sergeant stared down at Elsbeth. Suddenly he grinned, his hands gesturing wildly, breaking the language barrier. "Maybe you could mop some floors, make some beds. Work in the *hospital*." He was yelling now, as if that would make them understand better. "The little guy, he could run some errands for me when he gets better. *Ja? Ja?* How about it? *Ja?*"

Laughing and crying at once, Elsbeth nodded. Jaroslav and Emil nodded too, although they hadn't understood a word.

"Come on, I'm requisitioning you. Soldier, give the little guy a hand." Beckoning them, the sergeant led the way to the road. As they passed the nurses he grinned at them. "Meet your new staff."

Elsbeth, Emil and Jaroslav followed him, hardly daring to look at one another. The sergeant put the key in the ignition. Elsbeth held her breath, but the car started and she thought maybe she could trust him.

"When we get you to Wunsiedel, you kids better go to the canteen. Food, *ja?*" He held up the bone that was Elsbeth's arm. "You got to get some food in you. You look like three bean poles." He glanced back to make sure the soldier was returning to his post. "Where're you from, anyway?" he asked in a quiet voice.

Elsbeth stared back at him. This was a different kind of interrogation. She found it strange. "We come from Saaz," she answered in a low voice, a new strength flooding through her. "We come all alone. We did it ourselves." Suddenly filled with mistrust again, she began to babble. "Papers. We have our papers."

"Yeah. Okay. Take it easy, *ja?*" He patted her arm gently.

Ahead of them the nurses drove into an encampment of tents just outside the village. They stopped in front of the one with a huge red cross on the roof. The blonde one who'd yelled to the sergeant walked back to where their jeep had halted.

"What's it to be, kids? Hamburgers first? Or delousing first?" She smiled at them.

Elsbeth had heard how the only food Americans ever ate was hamburgers and hot dogs. The thought of meat filled her mouth with saliva and made her feel dizzy.

"Elsbeth! Elsbeth! Are you all right?" Jaroslav was bending over her.

"I'm okay." Elsbeth was astonished to find herself lying on the floor. "I must have fainted."

The blonde woman brought a warm cloth and began wiping her brow. "Poor little tyke," she said over and over.

"I am *not* a poor person." Elsbeth struggled to sit up. "*I* brought them all to freedom. *I* did it." Then suddenly remembering how Jaroslav came back, how he picked Emil up, she smiled right at him. "*We* did it."

"Yes," the nurse said quietly. "I understand. Do you have any family?"

"We meet Papa in Bayreuth. He comes from Czechoslovakia too. But by a different route."

"Give me his name. We can telephone Bayreuth to keep an eye out for him. Everyone contacts our unit sooner or later when they're looking for someone. They'll let us know as soon as he arrives. In the meantime, you'd better not get up just yet."

"*Nein, Fräulein.*" Elsbeth grabbed hold of Jaroslav and hauled herself to her feet, still dizzy. "We work for our supper. Canada? Fräulein tell us about Canada, *ja*? I would like to know all about this ice and snow country."

Part II

VISA TO CANADA

9

On a Mission

Don't let me slip under the wheels," prayed Jaroslav as, half hidden, he stood in the drizzle at the very end of the long railway platform. "Dear God, don't let me fall. Don't let the train cut my legs off."

He heard the conductor call for the last boarding. Grunting and squealing like a monster about to attack, the train he had chosen advanced towards him, pulling flatcars with metre-high metal walls around them out of Nuremberg.

Jaroslav crossed himself. As the puffing engine, the coal car and some freight cars passed in front of him, the train picked up speed. Suddenly he hurled himself at one of the flatcars. He heard himself screaming as he missed and fell towards the ground, towards the steel wheels, and his fingers scrabbled to grab hold of something, anything. A million years passed before his fingers, sliding along the lip of the metal wall, scraping skin, held on. His body thumping against the side of the train, in rhythm with its swaying, Jaroslav hung on for dear life. He struggled for a toehold.

"Got it!" he panted as one foot found a narrow metal ledge at the bottom of the flatcar. He inched that foot sideways and, resting his weight on it, hauled himself up till he straddled the wall. Blinking away his sweat, he looked down at the wheels as they clacked over the tracks. He shivered. "Hail Mary, full of Grace," he whispered as he lowered himself onto his hands and knees inside the car.

"Made it!" he breathed, his eyes now watering against the cinders floating back from the steam engine eight cars ahead.

He staggered to his feet and stood swaying with the motion of the train. He couldn't collapse, couldn't even sit down yet. Painstakingly, he brushed dust off the lodencoat and respectable suit he was wearing and started to straighten his tie, then hesitated, looking down at his dirty fingers caked with blood. Later, he thought, leaning over and buffing his leather shoes with the back of his hand.

"What a birthday," he growled as he tried to calm himself. "A man doesn't cry." *Today I am a man. Fifteen. Anyway, I did it — I got on board. Wait till Herr Hoffer hears how smart I was. He'll never believe I only bought a platform ticket instead of paying full price for a regular one. I was crazy to take such a chance. But now I'll have enough money left to get a meal in a proper restaurant.*

Jaroslav's fingers probed for the few bills Herr Hoffer had given him to last this long trip.

Stepping clear of some swirls of coal dust, he walked to the end of the empty boxcar. With his foot he cleared the black dust away. He unfolded a couple of pieces of newspaper that Elsbeth had given him to use as toilet paper, and he sat down and leaned back into the corner. He had been surprised to find no one else aboard his boxcar. Refugees by the millions were clogging the roads, making them heave and sway to the rumble of small carts and the walk of limping families. Yet he knew he would be joined before long by another Displaced Person just like him, and another and another, riding the rails.

His misery returned, and it occured to him that he didn't even know what direction he was travelling in. He stood up and looked out across the fields ploughed for fall planting, and at the little villages of West Germany, only a few kilometres apart. Everything looked grey in the light rain.

He hoped he was on his way north to the sea at Hamburg, but he knew that the Russian zone spearpointed into Germany like a giant finger, so he might be going west around it, far into the Rhineland, many kilometres out of his way.

"Happy Birthday to me," he muttered as he sat down again and angrily slammed his hand flat into the side of the boxcar, grimacing as he hurt himself. He longed for a journal, a sketchpad, anything to record how he was feeling.

Look at me, he chided himself. Here I am, huddled

under a plastic cape some American once owned to protect himself against chemical warfare. Jaroslav's hair, wet now, clung to his head, but he was grateful to Herr Hoffer for lending him the lodencoat he wore over his suit. At least tonight I won't freeze, he thought.

But Herr Hoffer was not his father. His own father right now was lighting candles for him, far away back home in Saaz. My home, he thought, his throat thickening with homesickness. I'll never see my Czechoslovakia again.

Struggling not to break down, Jaroslav focussed instead on Elsbeth's parting words. "You're not in danger," she'd said. "You won't get shot. If you get picked up by the police, we'll come and get you. Just bring back our money. You know we've got to have it to buy passage to Canada." Her voice had softened. "Papa's trying to get word out to your father. Maybe he'll defect. Who knows? If he does, he could come with us."

He sat up straighter. Have to stay awake, he thought, patting the piece of bread Elsbeth had tucked in his pocket.

I'm on a mission. He said this to himself over and over again. Herr Hoffer chose me to collect the family money. Me, an outsider. Me, who held back food from Herr Hoffer's daughter and son. Herr Hoffer didn't pick Elsbeth. He trusts me. He must think I can do it. With a start, Jaroslav checked to make sure he hadn't lost the envelope Herr Hoffer had given him. He knew he was exhausted, but the hollow feeling inside had nothing to do with that.

Jaroslav fought off sleep by biting his lip repeatedly. Herr Hoffer's face and his crinkly laugh lines kept reappearing in his memory. Jaroslav allowed himself to be comforted now, but when he thought back to three weeks ago . . . he remembered their reunion, he remembered how he had been angry, how he had been afraid . . .

"Emil! Give me that mop!" Elsbeth had yelled, chasing after her little brother, who was slipping and sliding along the freshly washed floor.

"Go get him, sister," yelled an "Ami" — as the Germans called American G.I.s — in English, gesturing wildly with his thumb towards the door.

"Ten to one says the little guy gets away," called an older man, twisting his bandaged head to watch.

"Ah, leave 'em alone," called another, with crutches beside his bed. "They ain't got no mother or father here."

Elsbeth cursed them all in German, while Jaroslav stood well back, laughing. The last few weeks of meat or fish every day, a job to do and a bed with clean sheets every night had been peaceful. Too peaceful for a seven-year-old, Jaroslav snickered as he watched Emil, cornered by a door too stubborn to open, defend himself by poking the mop handle first to Elsbeth's left and then to her right.

"Keep away. You're not my mother! I don't have to do what you say!" With that, Emil shoved the wet mop right into Elsbeth's face.

Elsbeth flushed with rage. Even with all the laughing and joking that had been going on in the recovery unit, the look on Emil's face told Jaroslav and everyone else that he knew he'd gone too far.

Jaws clenched, Elsbeth grabbed her brother by his wrists and dragged him to the closest empty bed. She plunked herself down and dragged him, stumbling, over her knee to spank him.

"*I am the boss.*" Elsbeth spat out each word as Emil kicked and yanked his arm, trying to get free. "You heard Mama when she left. You've been so good this last month, waiting for Papa. Why did you pick this week to be such a brat every single day?" She raised her hand and her tone hardened. "Nobody pushes a wet mop in my face and gets away with it."

Emil twisted around and screamed in German. "Papa's not coming! He's never coming. We're going to be stuck here forever with these strange Americans. We'll never get to Canada. Papa lied. And you're not the boss over me. You're not Mama. You and Jaroslav are telling me lies. If Papa's coming, where is he? Where is he?" Emil burst into tears.

"Here. I'm right here, son."

The words, loud and firm, halted Elsbeth's angry hand in midair and quieted the bedlam of the ward. A tall man with a moustache had yanked open the door that had been so stubbornly stuck a few moments before. Behind him stood one of the green-gowned American doctors.

"Papa," breathed Elsbeth so quietly Jaroslav could hardly hear her. "I don't believe it!"

Emil wriggled off her lap and catapulted into his father's arms. Elsbeth's legs buckled as she got up from the bed and it seemed to take forever for her to walk the few steps to her father.

"Oh Papa. It's you!" Still holding Emil, Herr Hoffer leaned towards his daughter as she threw her arms around his neck. "I knew you'd come. I knew it." Their cries and laughter seemed deafening in a ward that held its breath in silence.

Jaroslav felt choked with jealousy as he watched the three Hoffers kissing and chattering. He shied away from remembering his own father, so important as commissar back home and so absent here in the American hospital in Bayreuth.

What about me? he thought, lounging against the wall. What am I going to do now? What if Herr Hoffer doesn't want me? Elsbeth said I'd go to Canada with them. But she's not the boss anymore. Herr Hoffer was always fair when he was my father's boss, but he might not want me now.

I better look after myself, he reasoned, and began to rehearse in his head the best way to go about this. If only I spoke better English, he thought, I could tell this big American doctor that I, Jaroslav, can mop a floor better, can carry a tray better, can even fix a jeep better. I will try, he resolved, but not today. He turned away to leave the ward.

"Wait, Jaroslav," called Herr Hoffer, loosening himself from his children and striding down the aisle, his hand extended. "I heard about your bravery. The American sergeant told me how you went back and helped carry Emil across No Man's Land. We are honoured to have such a young man as part of our family." He shook Jaroslav's hand, and abruptly the boy felt himself gathered into the man's arms and held tightly. "You are with us now," Herr Hoffer said.

"Papa!" Elsbeth approached her father. "I have something to tell you. About Mama . . . She's . . . "

Herr Hoffer held up his hand. "Don't," he said, his face crumpling. "The sergeant already told me. Please. Don't talk about it now."

"Mama went to Russia," Emil called out. "But she's coming back."

Elsbeth stared at her father and slowly shook her head.

"Not now, children. We'll talk about Mama when we get settled."

Later that night, in the lounge beside the canteen, Herr Hoffer struggled to keep down the first solid food he'd eaten in two days. "This is a miracle." He grimaced, then smiled. "Do you know how many days I've been wandering around, pestering the police, inquiring at the train station, asking in every restaurant?" Although his eyes, deep-set from hunger, seemed piercing, he gazed longingly at his children.

"Why didn't you ask the Americans about us?" Elsbeth interrupted.

"That was the first place I went. But the soldier was reading a comic book. He barely glanced at the list and said he'd never heard of you." Herr Hoffer swore under his breath.

"Then I ran out of food. Earlier today I collapsed with sharp pains in my side and a stranger told everyone I had a burst appendix and they brought me to this hospital."

"Did you get cut open, Papa?" Emil wriggled in his chair.

"No. I was starving. I broke down in the doctor's office after he brought me a little food. I told him about losing all of you."

"He said, 'That's funny. Your children sound like the kids we've got working here.' Then he took me to your ward."

Elsbeth snuggled closer to her father on the couch. "Now we're all together, we can stay with the Americans. Maybe that doctor can help us get our visas to emigrate."

"Haw," Jaroslav scoffed. "Everybody wants to go to America. But nobody gets in."

Elsbeth made a face and stuck her tongue out at him. "*Dumkopf*. We're not going to America. We're going to Canada. And we're going to get in. We can work here and get lots of money." She twisted around to look right at her father. "Papa, I bet the Americans would give you a job too. Then we'd get to Canada sooner."

Her father leaned back and took a deep breath. "We can't stay here, Elsbeth. The Americans looked after you only because you told them I was coming. Now I'm here. We have to leave."

"But how will we eat?" Jaroslav felt panic rising in his throat as he recalled how desperate they had been for apples and bread when they were escaping to freedom. "There are so many homeless people begging from every cart out there." He could feel himself getting angry. "We're okay here. We should stay here."

"No!" Herr Hoffer answered sharply. "We can't stay here."

Jaroslav turned away. "We should stay here," he muttered again.

"I brought a little money out with me," Herr Hoffer continued. "The Russians paid me a stipend to show them how to get a paper plant operating. There are refugee depots where we can all get a little bread and some soup."

"Yeah. Stand in line for five lousy hours to get some coloured water with cockroaches in it," Jaroslav hurled over his shoulder as he walked over to the window.

"Jaroslav, we are all together. We are all alive. We are all safe. That's what counts." Herr Hoffer got up and crossed the room to put an arm around the boy. Jaroslav saw hamburgers and daily baths fade from his life and he didn't like it. But he knew he was afraid to stay here alone.

"Where are we going, Papa?" Emil's short legs swung back and forth, back and forth.

"Nuremberg."

"Nuremberg? Why, Papa?"

"Something important is already happening in Nuremberg. Whispers along the roads say it's the most important event in the history of the war. Because of its importance, a battalion of Canadians is stationed there."

"What is happening, Papa?"

"Later, later." Herr Hoffer smiled, picking Emil up in his arms. "Now we must all go to bed. Remember, the gateway to Canada is through Nuremberg."

Emil struggled to get loose. "Papa, you have to leave a note for Mama. You can leave it with the sergeant. It can tell her we've gone to Nuremberg. She knows we were supposed to come to Bayreuth. This is where she'll come when she escapes."

A sigh from deep inside Elsbeth forced her to look away. "Papa can leave a note," she mumbled. "It can say we've gone to Nuremberg."

Jaroslav frowned. "I thought Berlin was the gateway to Canada."

"Right now Berlin is divided into four zones: Russian, American, British and French. The war is barely over and no one knows for sure yet who has what. The Russians threw all of us into camps. They shipped Mama . . . " His voice broke and he turned away, holding Emil so tightly that the boy began to struggle. "I can't . . . I don't want . . . I'm never living like that again. So we stay away from Berlin." He shivered and set Emil down.

"Look, children. On my journey to find you, I heard from refugees on the road that Nuremberg is in good shape. They didn't think too many bombs fell there. And gossip says there's food."

"Everybody will head for Nuremberg right away and there won't be any food left," Jaroslav said scornfully.

"No worse than here. Canadians are in Nuremberg. You can talk to them, find out about what city we should go to. Maybe they'd even help us to get our visas to immigrate."

"Nobody's going to help us now that you're with us."

"Are you coming to Nuremberg or not, Jaroslav?" Herr Hoffer snapped.

"I guess I have to."

"Be positive, Jaroslav. We are alive. We're together. We'll be fine as long as we all stay together. The gateway to Canada is through Nuremberg. Now, away to sleep, all of you. Tomorrow I'll pay someone to take us in his truck to Nuremberg."

Nuremberg . . . Nuremberg . . . Nuremberg . . .

Jaroslav woke to the slow, heavy side-to-side sway that told him he'd better be on guard. The whistle was blowing, and he suspected that the engineer was stopping to take on more coal and water to drive the steam engine.

Getting to his feet, he peered warily through the fog. The drizzle had let up and a murky light showed him four empty trains parked side by side on the sidings, waiting to refill. Jaroslav ran his tongue over his parched lips. I bet there's a tap at that maintenance shed, he thought.

As quietly as he could, he climbed the wall of the flatcar and, not seeing any train officials, dropped to the ground and flattened himself. He became aware of rounded shapes in the darkness, crawling towards the train. One or two of them hauled themselves on board cars farther down the track. More refugees like me, Jaroslav thought, relaxing. They're a lot smarter than I was. They wait till the train is stopped and they can climb on board the easy way.

He wiggled along the ground, rolled over one track and under the first train, then along and under the next. Thank God for this plastic cape, he thought. It'll protect my suit. He could hear the conductor in the distance talking to his engineer. Jaroslav rolled under the third train. Just one more to go, he thought as he lay on the cinders.

Suddenly a window opened right above him. Jaroslav pressed himself against the dirt and gravel. "Just emptying the slops," a man called out above him as a bucket of toilet waste splattered his plastic cape with full force.

Jaroslav grunted, clenching his teeth to keep from yelling at the imbecile. He was so mad he didn't bother any more with hiding. He jumped to his feet and strode around the last train to the maintenance shed.

Around one corner of the shed, he found the tap. First he washed off his cape, scrubbing to get it clean. From behind came the sounds of a train getting ready to leave. He cursed quietly and shook out the cape. He sniffed it and was satisfied that it was clean.

When he had rinsed his hands repeatedly, he leaned forward and drank deeply. Then, doubled over, he hurried back to his flatcar.

"Here, boy, I give you a hand," a voice whispered in halting German. But as Jaroslav threw one leg over the side, he felt himself shoved back, falling, falling, as the train began to roll.

10

All the Way to Nuremburg

Jaroslav jumped to his feet and ran alongside the train. He leaped up onto a freight car and climbed aboard as the train rolled out.

The vague shapes lying or sitting nearby were indifferent to whether he made it on board. But from the moment he had been shoved he knew he had to be on guard. True, he had hardly any money. But others had none. And what he had, he needed. He kept close watch, but the others were exhausted too, and he was soon able to doze off.

The next morning it hit home. Without a train ticket, he could be thrown in jail if either the conductor or the police spotted him hopping on board any trains that were stopped or shunting before they pulled out.

Irritable and feeling unrested, he wished he'd stolen another piece of bread before he'd left Elsbeth. Through the next days and nights travelling west to Stuttgart, it seemed to him that when he wasn't sitting cramped or wet, he was lining up for watery soup in transit camps.

"There's a good hostel in Hamburg when you get there," one man told him as they both stood in a queue for food.

A woman wearing three sweaters and two skirts offered, "Hamburg is no good. What do you go to Hamburg for? Stop when you get to Hanover. In Hanover there is food. Be smart, stay in Hanover. My cousin sent word it is good in Hanover."

"Just outside Stuttgart is where you have to jump the train to Hanover," said another man, chewing on his pipestem. "The train faces the overpass and will pull out that way. Watch for the overpass. Have you heard if there's any tobacco on the black market here?"

In bits and perks, for the next four days, Jaroslav slept and hid and tried to find water all the way north to Hanover, a journey that normally took only half a day from Nuremberg.

Exhausted, he tumbled off the train in the dead of night, frantic to find a place to sleep. I'll get rousted by the police if I sleep outside the station or in the hallways without a train ticket, he thought. Where can I go? What'll I do? Once again he checked inside his pocket where Herr Hoffer's letter rested. Herr Hoffer has trusted me to get his money. I've got to think of something.

He headed down the stairs, down into the sub-basement, deep below the station where the toilets were. Rounding the corner, he reeled under the stench that filled the place.

He halted, struggling not to cry. Thin, gaunt shapes, coughing and snoring, all wearing as many clothes as they could, crushed together on the benches. Three women, arms around each other so as not to fall off, slept on top of a trestle table.

Jaroslav, swaying, almost unable to breathe, knew he would never make it back upstairs, knew there was no place else to sleep where he wouldn't get arrested.

"Pardon me, excuse me," he muttered as he dropped to his knees and forced his way along the floor, over boots, in and around legs, till he collapsed beneath the table. Choked, trying not to breathe deeply, Jaroslav wished with all his heart he had never gone with the Hoffers to Nuremberg. Nuremberg, he thought bitterly as he closed his eyes. Herr Hoffer's dream was Nuremberg . . .

"Elsbeth! Emil! Jaroslav! Eat up! We're leaving at seven, before the roads get too clogged." Herr Hoffer had bustled into the cafeteria where the children were eating breakfast. "Be sure and bring the plastic capes you were given. Wear as many warm clothes as you can. Don't carry them. They could get stolen. Don't forget to say goodbye to the sergeant and the doctor and the head nurse."

"We have to leave a note for Mama with the sergeant." Emil held out his hand. "Give me a pencil, Elsbeth."

Elsbeth stared at him. "Stop it, Emil. I don't believe Mama's — "

"Of course we'll leave a note. No harm in leaving word." Papa passed a pencil to Elsbeth as he gave a slight shake with his head.

"What about food?" Jaroslav had never adjusted to the lack of food the way Elsbeth and Emil had been forced to do in the camp.

Herr Hoffer hesitated. "I don't have much money left. We need it for Nuremberg."

"Never mind, Papa," Elsbeth spoke up. "The cook here has been good to us. I'll get some cheeseburgers. Emil, you go and get as much butter as you can. We can use it to trade for other things. Jaroslav, you try for bread, powdered milk and some hard boiled eggs." She turned to her father, who was looking at her with a startled expression. "Do we need anything else, Papa?"

Herr Hoffer took his daughter's hand and raised it to his lips. "I kiss your hand in admiration, Elsbeth. You use your wits to survive."

Jaroslav clenched his teeth. You use your wits to survive, he mimicked in his head. You use your wits to survive. *I* could have thought of all those things. She just spoke up first. But all he said was, "I'm going to get the eggs. Where do we meet?"

"At the front doors of the hospital administration building. I found a driver who is a cousin of one of the men who used to work for me in the plant back home in Saaz."

Half an hour later Herr Hoffer and the children sat shivering slightly in the crisp October air, waiting. They played ball and waited, played tag and waited. Finally at eleven o'clock an old truck with a heavy tarpaulin thrown over the back lumbered up. A short man with a scar across one cheek jumped out and greeted Herr Hoffer.

Jaroslav watched them. The driver's eyes never seemed to meet Herr Hoffer's. They looked to the ground or off to one side. I don't trust him, he thought, as the man walked around to the back of the truck and, staring down at the road, held up the tarp for them all to crawl under.

But Herr Hoffer shook his head. "I ride in the front with you," he said quietly, walking up front and opening the passenger door of the cab.

Lying under the khaki tarpaulin, Jaroslav relaxed. He liked the oily smell of the heavy fabric and began to feel Herr Hoffer was right. In Nuremberg there would be a place to live. He suspected that Herr Hoffer would start up another big business and save enough money to be able to live in style in Canada.

He must have slept for a long time before angry voices woke him. Elsbeth put her finger to her lips, listening, as Emil stirred from sleep. The truck, which had been driven, in low gear, in and around the refugees cluttering the road, shuddered to a stop, between nothing but fields of stubble.

"Give me your jacket! I want the children's sweaters or I go no farther!" Jaroslav hopped out of the back to see what was happening. The driver looked menacing as he jumped out of the cab onto the well-used road. "Your money only takes you this far. You can walk from here," he gestured, "like them."

Herr Hoffer's voice rose in anger. "I paid triple what it would take to get us to Nuremberg. *All the way to Nuremberg.*"

Jaroslav called from where he was standing. "Here. Take this." He pulled off his sweater and held it out. "How many . . . say . . . eggs would it take to get us to Nuremberg?"

The man looked crafty. "Eggs? You have eggs?"

"Shhhhh, not so loud." Jaroslav, who'd come up to the man, gestured towards the silent line of refugees. Herr Hoffer, still thin and weak, had joined them. "Don't do it, Jaroslav. We need those eggs."

"Four?" Jaroslav persisted. "Would four be enough?"

"No. Four wouldn't do it." The man spat on the ground. "Get on your way. This truck goes no farther."

"How many eggs will get us to Nuremberg?"

"How many have you got?"

Jaroslav sighed deeply. Out of all his various pockets, he produced six eggs. The driver stepped close to him and ran his hands over Jaroslav's body, to make sure he didn't have any more hidden away. Jaroslav peeled off his sweater and held it out. "Elsbeth!" he called back to where she was standing, an arm around Emil, frightened. "Give him your sweater. Emil's too."

Hands shaking with restrained anger, Herr Hoffer wrenched off his tweed jacket and handed it over. He quickly stepped behind the driver and pushed him roughly back into the cab. "You've robbed us of our food and warmth. Now you take us *all the way to Nuremberg.*" He clasped Jaroslav around the shoulder. "Thanks. Get in, children," he yelled, running round to the passenger side and jumping in himself.

Jaroslav lingered a moment, and he overheard Herr Hoffer say quietly: "I never forget a face, my friend. You watch out that we don't meet again when *you* need *me*."

As Jaroslav jumped in, Elsbeth hissed, "Where did you hide the rest of the eggs?" Grinning, Jaroslav pointed to the centre of a huge coil of rope beside him. As the truck began to slowly lumber forward again, Jaroslav took out a pencil he'd been given and began to sketch, very roughly, on the floor of the truck, some of the carts and families they were passing.

Elsbeth watched him. "I didn't know you could draw," she said.

"I can't." He shrugged as the jousting of the truck threw every line askew . . .

Jaroslav woke suddenly to querulous, anxious voices from the front cab. He glanced out and recognized the outskirts of Nuremberg. He leaped up and began folding the tarpaulin back. "Wake up, Elsbeth. We're here. This is our gateway to — "

His mouth fell open as the truck carried them relentlessly into Nuremberg. "It's rubble," he finally cried, "nothing but rubble." We can't trust rumours, he thought. No one, not even Herr Hoffer, knows anything for sure. We're all adrift. We've no one; nothing to hang on to. Nothing is real.

Nuremberg had been bombed to the ground. Refugees scuttled here and there, scavenging for bricks left whole in the bombing to build a little shelter. A child squatted for warmth in front of a small fire. In the distance, Jaroslav could see small clutches of buildings, such as the Palace of Justice, that had been spared.

"I got you to Nuremberg." Jaroslav heard the evil triumph in the driver's voice. "Going to start a little business, are you? Going to live higher on the hog than the rest of us peasants, are you?" The driver shrieked with laughter. "Herr Hoffer, *you* will never have anything more *I* would want. You won't survive a week here."

Nuremberg . . . laughter . . . mocking . . . smell . . . a horrible sme — Jaroslav gagged as one leg locked in a cramp and jolted him awake. I am not travelling like this anymore, he thought, disoriented. Even if it costs the last deutsche mark Herr Hoffer gave me.

He backed out from under the table and went into the toilet. He felt funny and found himself giggling and talking to himself as he washed. The stench nauseated him and he tried not to breathe as he brushed his suit and said again a prayer of thankfulness for his plastic cape. The other men looked nervous, and he was shocked to find himself grinning at them in the mirror.

Upstairs in the Hanover train station he pressed his lips together so as not to babble as he bought himself a train ticket. The moment he boarded the passenger car he could hardly believe his eyes.

He had stepped into a past that existed only before the war. Here were other men in business suits, obviously prosperous, and women wearing fashionable hats. Most of the passengers were members of the German navy, discharged from duty but still wearing their uniforms. Jaroslav was sure everyone was staring at him. He struggled to keep back a flood of strange, inappropriate questions. Do I smell of toilets? he wanted to ask. Is there dirt on my face? I must be mad, he thought.

"We're all penned up just around the foot of Denmark, my friend," a talkative sailor confided in German after shifting over so Jaroslav could sit down. "We've got to wait — see what they'll do with us, now they've defeated us." He gestured towards the road outside. "At least our officers are travelling in style, even though all our weapons have been taken away." A German staff car with naval officers sitting in the back was riding abreast of the train and two more were in the distance. Lorries loaded with British soldiers were also crowding the roads.

Jaroslav must have dozed off again because he didn't even notice the train had arrived in Hamburg. "Wake up, mate," the sailor called out, waving goodbye.

Jaroslav stood so quickly he felt dizzy, and he staggered out of the train onto a swaying platform. He clung to the station walls, as he slowly made his way out onto the street. He just made it to the gutter when he began to retch.

"There, there, my boy. Go to it. Nothing's coming up." The elderly woman who had been limping along behind him patted his shoulders gently. "Here. This is all I can spare. Wait till the heaves are over." She took some bread from her pocket and tore off a small piece for Jaroslav. "God go with you," she blessed as she walked away, her cane tapping against the cobblestones.

"Thank you," Jaroslav whispered hoarsely as his body stopped shaking. I'm not insane, he almost cried out. I'm just delirious from no food. He slid down onto the cobblestones and waited until his stomach settled. Then he nibbled the bread.

He wanted to sit there forever, but he heard a bell chime. I forgot, he thought. This is Friday. It's late. Got to find the commuter train. Got to get to the factory before it closes. He struggled to his feet, forcing himself to focus enough to re-enter the station.

He dragged himself along the platform to board the train that would carry him out to the suburbs. As he settled into his seat, he began to worry whether the factory would still be open. He re-called his last talk with Herr Hoffer before he had set out.

"I'm not going to tell you how to collect the money, Jaroslav," Herr Hoffer had said. "But this Herr Director has paid all his bills except this last one. He knows that he owes us this money. I'm giving you a letter to present to him. You think quickly in an emergency. I have to trust you with this important task. We're desperate for money to live — to get to Canada. We'll leave word where we'll be when you get back. Remember, don't lose the letter." Herr Hoffer had clapped him on the back and smiled. Jaroslav began to believe that he could succeed at such an important mission.

"Wait! Wait!" he called as he hurried towards the

factory gates a couple of blocks from the commuter station. They clanged shut just as he got there.

"Come back Monday," the porter said, turning away.

"No! Wait! I've come all the way from Nuremberg. I have an appointment with Herr Director," Jaroslav lied. "He said for me to go to his home if I arrived too late."

"Well . . . he left just five minutes ago." The man hesitated, taking note of Jaroslav's suit. "You're obviously dressed for business. These days nothing runs on time, not even the trains. I guess it's all right to give his address to you."

When he learned that the director lived in yet another suburb, ten kilometres away, Jaroslav stared in despair at the porter.

He knew it would take his last shred of strength to get there. Then, stubbornly, he put one foot in front of another and another and another, and he progressed block after block in a daze. After a couple of kilometres he could feel his feet swelling, pressing viciously against his ill-fitting leather shoes. In a way, he was grateful. The pain brought his mind down from somewhere outside himself where it had been floating.

Dizzy, and unable to focus clearly, Jaroslav at last found the director's home — a perfect little house with curtains and a small stone wall around a garden with fruit trees. Jaroslav felt a deep stab of envy as he banged the knocker.

The director looked angry as he opened the door. "What do you want?" he demanded.

Jaroslav stared at a stout, well-fed man. In that moment he couldn't tell whether dealing with the director would be easy or difficult. "I've come to collect the money that is owed to Herr Hoffer." Jaroslav willed himself to stand as straight as he could and to speak clearly. He found himself swaying anyway, and he was embarrassed.

"Come back Monday. You know this is the weekend. We're closed."

Jaroslav knew better than to betray his despair. When you want something from someone you don't let him know you're starving, he reasoned, attempting a slight formal bow. "Monday it is, Herr Director," he said, wondering if he would faint here or at the end of the garden.

The director stared piercingly at Jaroslav. "Wait here," he ordered and slammed the door.

Jaroslav didn't care about anything as he tried not to fall.

Before long the door swung open. "Here. Some pears from the garden," the director said gruffly, holding out a brown paper bag. "Eat them slowly. Very slowly. Just half a one now. Half a one in an hour. Come on Monday to my office." Again he slammed the door.

11

Appointment with the Director

*J*aroslav felt as though his calves and feet were strong as steel as, clear-headed once more, he marched the many kilometres back into Hamburg.

Clutching the bag of pears, he had groped his way out of the director's garden, until, hidden by a tree, he had wolfed down the lot. His stomach had heaved slightly, but the pears had stayed down as he rested for a while.

A man doesn't get his life handed back to him every day, he thought, feeling cocky as he strode along. I'm going to celebrate. Jaroslav knew that if he was in an area for any length of time he was required to get a ration card. But no one would ask him for one in the dining room of a good hotel. So he inquired along the way and was directed to a first-class one.

When he arrived, he brushed off his suit and,

holding himself erect, followed the maitre d' to his table. Jaroslav pretended he was some rich businessman and sat with his chin held high.

"Tonight, sir, we have caviar sandwiches and two per cent beer only to drink." Jaroslav nodded automatically, though he felt intimidated. Caviar, he thought, I've never tasted fish eggs before. But this is a celebration — I should try something new. At the first bite, he was deeply disappointed. Caviar tasted as familiar as Friday-night fish.

"Ground herring, young man." A man at the next table, who looked important even in his threadbare clothes, leaned towards Jaroslav and held out his plate. "Would you like mine too? There's too much salt in it. I can't eat it."

Jaroslav thanked him and polished off the man's plate. He sat back, feeling full for the first time since he'd left the cafeteria in the American hospital. "I need somewhere to sleep," he said. "Have you heard of any good places?"

"If you don't pass out when they bring you the bill for this disgusting meal, I suggest you try a good hostel out in the eastern suburbs." The man pulled down his vest as he rose to leave. "Don't worry. It only takes a bit of change to get out there by subway. Listen, this is how you go."

As he left to hunt for the address, Jaroslav won dered if the hostel would be good or if he'd end up in some kind of fleabag. He was so thirsty on the way that he had to get off the subway three times to find a drinking fountain.

He located the street and rounded the corner.

"*Mein Gott*," he said. He was looking up at a huge, exclusive spa and bathing establishment surrounded by an ornate garden. "Is this my hostel?"

"Come in, come in," boomed an attendant, beckoning Jaroslav to follow him into the former club for the rich, now taken over by the State. Marble baths and what had been hot tubs were sunken everywhere in between huge massage tables that erupted out of the marble floors.

There were dozens of small cubicles where once people had changed, and Jaroslav assumed that was where he would sleep. But the attendant kept going until finally he pointed. "This is for you," he said.

The laugh began deep in Jaroslav's chest and almost choked him. In front of him lay an elegant pink marble bathtub. Wait till Herr Hoffer hears how I spent my first night in Hamburg, he thought. No rubble or fleas for me tonight! He climbed onto the mattress in the tub, pulled the blankets up and had his first good night's sleep since he had left the Hoffers.

Saturday and Sunday stretched long and empty before him when he woke up, a knot of worry pinching his stomach. I'll go sightseeing, he decided, just like a tourist. (Jaroslav knew Hamburg had so many canals it was known as the Venice of the North.) On Monday I'm not going to fail. The director will pay me what he owes Herr Hoffer. Elsbeth will never be able to throw it in my face that she could have done better, he thought, going next door for some bread and soup.

Excited now, Jaroslav rode to the end of the

Hamburg public transit line to see the huge port, an arm with many fingers for berthing more than 500 ships. The docks stretched far out, reaching into the mouth of the Elbe, just six hours from the North Sea. Born inland, he'd never been as close to an ocean and didn't know what to expect. But ships for Canada leave from here, he reminded himself. I'll see as much as I can. I'll talk to everyone. Then I can take all the latest news about sailing dates to Herr Hoffer.

But he stepped off the tram into chaos. Three ships' horns were bellowing so loudly he had to cover his ears. Hundreds of emigrants called back over their shoulders as they either waited for or mounted gangplanks. Their ship was docked behind the old railway bridge. Relatives and friends were weeping and waving. High above them all were the offices of the Port Authority. A small military band played sad folk tunes as a send-off for those leaving the homeland, and Jaroslav began to feel so sad he hardly noticed himself scratching at the salt film formed by an inland ocean breeze on his face and hands.

Feeling a lump in his throat, he longed to write about or draw what he was seeing, and wished that he had pencil and paper. Confused, and unable to ask for gossip or news, he went back to the hostel to sleep in his pink marble bathtub again.

The next day, Sunday, the ships, the wide mouth of the Elbe, the ocean gateway to the people leaving and the ones left behind, drew him like a magnet. He sat quietly on a huge iron cleat at a remote dock, listening to the swell and ebb of the water.

These people are just like us, he thought. They want to get out of Germany. But when they leave they'll never see their families or friends again. I might never see my own father again, and he's only eight hundred kilometres away. He felt tears rush to his eyes. What will I do when we have the Atlantic Ocean between us? He felt so depressed that even the sight that night of his solid marble pink bathtub couldn't lift his spirits.

The next morning Jaroslav was shocked when he arrived at the gates and saw the size of the director's company. It stretched over four city blocks, like Herr Hoffer's had at home in Saaz. But now one half of the factory compound was occupied by British troops.

His voice was businesslike but his spirits were sinking as he was admitted by the guard and taken by the executive secretary into Herr Director's office.

"What can I do for you, young man?" Herr Director impatiently drummed his fingers on his desk. "Mondays are busy. Be as brief as you can."

"As I said on Friday, Herr Director, I'm here on behalf of Herr Hoffer." Jaroslav reached in his pocket and presented the letter from Elsbeth's father. "Your company has not paid its last bill to Hoffer Incorporated. The money is still owed. I'm here to collect it." Jaroslav spoke more loudly than usual, hoping that would give his words more authority. "Herr Hoffer has informed me that you know the law. If a private company is owed money, the money must be paid to the owner within the month."

Jaroslav took a deep breath. It's now or never, he thought. "The amount owed is stated in the letter, 68,000 deutsche marks. Herr Hoffer requests a bank draft, not a cheque."

"I'm waiting." The director sounded impatient again.

"For what?"

"For proof, young man. Where's your invoice?"

"I . . . I . . . " Jaroslav began to improvise, to stifle his panic. "Herr Hoffer said you would produce a copy of the invoice from your Accounts Department." His fingers explored his pockets. "I know mine must be here somewhere . . . I seem to have mislaid — "

The director interrupted. "Phone Accounting, Miss Schmidt," he called out to his secretary. "Find out if we owe anything to Hoffer Incorporated."

While they waited, Jaroslav stood staring down at the director, who shuffled his papers, cleared his throat and avoided looking up at the boy. Eventually the secretary stepped into the office.

"The invoice shows that nothing is owed to Hoffer Incorporated, Herr Director," she announced and left.

Smiling, showing him out the door, arm around Jaroslav's shoulder, the director was smug. "How were the pears? Good? Come again if you are in Hamburg. You see how hospitable we are. Come any time."

Jaroslav was stunned. Herr Hoffer had said the company would have a copy of the invoice showing that they owed the 68,000 deutsche marks. The law was the law, he'd said. Anyway, he'd said, Herr Director had paid all his other bills, so there should be no trouble. Jaroslav knew as well as Herr Director did that Herr Hoffer's copy sat far away back in Saaz in the Russian zone. But why would Herr Hoffer send him all this way if no money was owed?

Suddenly Jaroslav smelled a rat. Why didn't the secretary bring the invoice up to the office and show it to me? he wondered. She didn't even show a copy to Herr Director. I know he received that bill and never paid it.

Furious at how stupid he'd been, Jaroslav started to walk towards the gate to leave the factory compound, then changed his mind. He took out the worn English phrase book, the one he himself had rebound in wine leather in Herr Hoffer's factory during the war, and approached a scrawny British sergeant leaning against a wall.

"Good day . . . How . . . are . . . you?" He smiled and waited.

"'Allo, mate. Wotcher?"

"Me." He pointed to himself. "Speak English . . . to you . . . *ja?*" Jaroslav held up the phrase book.

"Righto, mate. Carry on. I'm on me break."

Haltingly, Jaroslav struggled to tell the older man how he had been cheated. How he had failed. How there was no money now to go to Canada. How Herr Director had lied.

"'E's a slimy one, that one. Listen, matey, 'op on back inter there." Jaroslav's spirits soared. He actually understood every word. He had never understood what the Americans had been talking about the whole time he'd been with them. But he understood this man. "'Ere, I'll 'old yer coat, so's you'll be just another employee, like, wearin' yer suit. 'Op it to Accounts. Give 'em whatfer. Get 'old o' the invoice yerself." The sergeant clapped Jaroslav on the back as he helped him off with his cape and lodencoat. "Wait for yer 'ere, mate."

Jaroslav's suit made him look like any other employee as he wended his way through the offices until he found Accounts. "Herr Director sent me to duplicate the Hoffer Incorporated accounts," he said to the receptionist. "Can I use that typewriter over there?" He pointed to an empty desk. The girl nodded and brought him the invoices.

Jaroslav's heart beat wildly as his fingers sought the outstanding bill. Yes, it says Hoffer Incorporated, he thought. Yes, the amount billed to Herr Director is 68,000 marks. No, there's no stamp saying it was paid. Got him! Jaroslav felt wonderful. He could hardly restrain himself from yelling and tossing all the papers up in the air.

He picked and pounded one finger at a time until the invoice was duplicated. He kept the original and handed back the duplicate. He marched back through the corridors and outside to reclaim his coat.

"*Danke schön*. You are a good man." Jaroslav hesitated, "I can not . . . "

"Forget it, mate. I'm on me way to Canada m'self. Down below in the mines I'm goin' like me pa." He gestured towards the factory with his thumb. "Slimy toad. You give 'im whatfer and I'll see yer across on t'other side. Buy me a cuppa in Canada." Giving Jaroslav the V for Victory sign, the sergeant waved goodbye.

"I need to see Herr Director again," Jaroslav said firmly to the secretary. He was wearing his coat again and carrying his cape as if he had just come back inside this minute.

As the secretary led him back into Herr Director's office he held the invoice aloft. "I have found my proof, Herr Director," he said loudly, heart beating wildly as he sat down. "You will see your records show the same, if you can find them." *I've got him. He's got to pay now.* Jaroslav could feel the money in his hand, could see himself travelling first class to Canada away from all this confusion and grime.

The director weighed the situation and then lied smoothly. "I found your invoice but unfortunately you had already gone." He leaned back and cleared his throat. "However, I don't have to pay this debt. It was incurred during the war. Now the war is over. The Allied armies have ordered all foreign debts to be registered with them. You must claim your money from them."

Jaroslav stood. "That isn't true! You owe Herr Hoffer 68,000 marks. *You must pay him.*" His voice almost broke, he was shaking so much. "The Hoffers are *starving* back in Nuremberg. Herr Hoffer gave me his last mark to come here. He believed you would honour your debt. I've come all this way! I have no money even for a train ticket back to Nuremberg!"

Herr Director was silent, but he looked ashamed. Then he got up. "I must talk to my legal department. You come back in two days."

Proud that he had stood up for himself, Jaroslav finally admitted he was a long way from collecting Herr Hoffer's money. I'm not beaten yet, though, he thought as he headed directly for the building where the authorities gave out food stamps to refugees. Afterwards, if he was lucky and found a store that actually had a little food to sell, these stamps would allow him to buy some.

As he walked block after block, it hit him how ordered everything was now, so soon after the war had ended. I just have to ask where the hostels are, he thought, where I go to get food stamps, where the refugee transit camps are, and I'm looked after by the State.

Though he knew he should have felt comforted by this, the streets of rubble, the distended stomachs of starving people, the blank stares of refugees who had given up made him afraid of what could happen to him.

The line-up at the food stamp building was long, and Jaroslav took his place behind a gaunt-looking man also wearing a business suit. He took out his phrase book, as he stood waiting, and began practising English.

Until he began coughing, he hadn't noticed the

dustman way ahead, sweeping up plaster and dust from a bomb crater in the middle of the building. As the line moved forward, swirling clouds of dust surrounded and settled on them. Jaroslav was dismayed.

Finally there were just the businessmen and Jaroslav left. I'll be out of here in two minutes, Jaroslav thought. Abruptly the clerk rose, slammed shut the bottom half of the door and took out her lunch and her knitting.

"*Nein, nein, Fräulein,*" the man ahead of Jaroslav shouted, shaking his finger at her as he marched into her office. "I have been waiting all morning. You have deliberately made the line move too slowly, just to fill in the time. You look after us right now. There are only two of us left."

Without a word, the woman packed up her lunch and her knitting. The man, thinking she was going to look after him, stepped out of her office. She smiled slightly as she too stepped out, slammed shut both halves of the door, locked them and left the building.

Jaroslav felt like killing the stupid man. Now they both sat, looking like dustmen themselves in the empty building, praying the woman would come back today. He's ruined our chances, Jaroslav thought, gritting his teeth. I can't do anything. He slumped, then began to wonder . . . I'll talk to her nicely, he decided, rehearsing in his head what he would say. I'll get her to like me. I can catch more flies with honey than with vinegar. Too bad that *dumkopf* didn't know that.

Two and a half hours later, sneezing from the plaster dust that had settled on his face as well, Jaroslav reached the wicket. The woman had come back and opened up again. Jaroslav smiled at her and explained how he had come all this way to deal with the huge chemical company run by Herr Director.

"*Ja*," she said. "They are pigs. *Mein* brother work for them ten years before the war. Now he limps from shrapnel so they don't give him a job." She *tsk-tsk*ed, and instead of giving Jaroslav two days' worth of food stamps, she handed him enough to last a week. She smiled. Jaroslav smiled back. Both knew he could barter the ones he didn't use.

He was amazed at himself. Now he knew what Elsbeth meant when she accused him of looking after himself. He saw that he hadn't just survived this, he had come out on top. And I'll beat Herr Director too, he thought.

Jaroslav felt just fine. Now I can buy a piece of cheese, if I can find some in a store, he thought. I can even go into an ordinary restaurant and order soup, potatoes and little bits of fish. He knew the restaurateurs collected the stamps from customers and used them to buy fish and chicken bones from wholesalers.

But as he wandered, passing canal after canal, looking for a stall or shop that might sell some cheese or an egg, he found nothing. When it began to grow dark, Jaroslav headed far from Lake Alster in the centre of Hamburg into a black-market district. I'll find a whole loaf of bread at least, he thought. He knew it would cost him his last pfennig to pay the expensive black-market prices, but still he asked directions to the seedy area, glancing over his shoulder as he approached.

"Diamonds for sale. A real bargain, my boy. Genuine diamonds." A man about eighty, leaning on a cane, held out an exquisite pair of earrings. "I gave them to my wife when we were marri . . . "

Jaroslav was horrified to see tears falling down the old man's cheeks, and he began to back away. A bony hand grabbed at the sleeve of his suit and tried to pull him back. "We have no money for food," the old man gasped. "We lived on bread and soup for the last five months. She's sick . . ." He let go of Jaroslav and turned away.

Depression choked Jaroslav as he realized he was the youngest person there. He couldn't wait to get out of the area, and hurried in the opposite direction, almost bumping into an elderly woman. She was heroically trying to sell a rough handmade broom to earn money for food. "My leg," she pointed. "I can't walk to the transit camp. I'm starving."

Without warning a whistle shrieked, trucks full of civilian and military police thundered up, and all the old people, who seemed to be the only vendors, stumbled over each other as they tried to escape and still hold on to the items they had been trying to sell.

Terrified, Jaroslav looked all around. He spotted a cheap pub for merchant seamen across the canal.

Those places are often raided, he thought, so it's probably got a back exit.

Quickly weaving his way through the crowd of frail, elderly survivors, Jaroslav prayed he wouldn't snap someone's limb in his rush. These survivors were all suffering from malnutrition, and he'd heard that their bones sometimes broke from just a shove.

I can't go to jail, he thought as he pulled open the pub door and dashed through it and out the back onto the next street. Abruptly he stopped running and attempted to whistle, his hands in his pockets, as if he were only out for an evening's stroll.

His pink marble bathtub had never looked so good as when he jumped into it that night.

The next morning, Jaroslav stared at himself in the mirror as he washed. Just one more day to go, he thought. But I've got to be careful. I can't trust anyone. The horror of last night's scene, the young military officers routing harmless, starving old people, haunted him.

I wish Elsbeth was here to tell me off, he thought. Remember, Jaroslav, you're here for one thing only. To get the money to go to Canada.

Exhausted after walking around the beautiful smaller Lake Alster, Binnenalster, in downtown Hamburg, Jaroslav decided to splurge in a café. It had once been popular — before one wall had collapsed during the bombing. He sat beside a prosperous-looking businessman.

"Are you in Hamburg seeing someone off?" the

man asked, offering Jaroslav a section of his newspaper to read.

"Not exactly," Jaroslav mumbled, feeling more and more like a failure. "I'm here to collect money."

"This is not an easy thing to do." The man shrugged. "I'm an industrialist and I know all about trying to collect money."

Before he knew it, Jaroslav's whole story had tumbled out, and he sat feeling drained.

"In my case, young man, a company here owes me millions, and I've been sitting here three weeks trying to get them to cough up. I'm not going to see a nickle of it."

Cursing himself for babbling to a stranger, Jaroslav ate quickly and left. The whole day he worried himself sick that the man might himself be trying to collect from Herr Director's company, might go to Herr Director and serve his own ends by prejudicing the company against paying the money to Jaroslav. Over and over he reminded himself of something he had learned in school: "Speech is the gift of all but thought is the gift of few."

Back at the factory the next morning, Herr Director announced, "My lawyer tells me I'm *not* to pay this debt." He avoided looking directly at Jaroslav but shuffled his papers continuously on his desk. "But I know you have to get back to Nuremberg, so I've instructed my secretary to give you a voucher to collect some cash from our payroll department. Business in Germany is so confused right now. Take my advice and go on home this afternoon."

Choked with hatred for Herr Director and frustrated by his own failure, Jaroslav left the factory with his skimpy payoff. I was trusted to go on this mission, he thought. I've failed Herr Hoffer. I've failed myself. How can we live in Nuremberg with no money. We'll never get to Canada now. Because of me we'll all be stuck here forever. Elsbeth was right. I can't be trusted.

My lawyer tells me . . . My lawyer tells me . . . Jaroslav mimicked Herr Director as he clenched his fist looking for something to punch. Lawyer . . . Lawyer . . . "Wait a minute! That's what I need," he said aloud. "A lawyer."

Running as fast as he could back to his elegant spa, he asked a couple of businessmen who were staying there, "Who's the best commercial lawyer in Hamburg?"

Half an hour later, Jaroslav found himself in a lawyer's office, anxiously waiting after he had told his story and produced the invoice.

"You have an excellent case, young man. Take these papers my secretary typed up to Nuremberg for Herr Hoffer to sign. Have him mail them back to me. We're going to sue Herr Director. Your 68,000 marks will be in your pocket in two or three months."

12

In Business at Last

I did it! Jaroslav patted the breast pocket where the lawyer's papers rested. Maybe I haven't got the actual cash, but this is as good as cash. He stared out the window of the passenger car, knowing that with his proper train ticket, his journey back to Nuremberg would be long but straightforward. He leaned his head back and tried to sleep.

Late the next morning, when he disembarked at Nuremberg and began to search for the villa of Herr Hoffer's friend, he felt bleak. At last he found the old metal shed in the yard of a vacant factory where the Hoffers had been forced to stay. "How can you stay here? There are holes in the roof! It's been raining nearly every day since I left. How did you stay dry?"

"We didn't." Elsbeth stood up and shivered, the cement floor cold and hard against her feet. "I hope Emil doesn't get sick. Did you get the money?"

"Don't tell me we all have to sleep on that!"

Jaroslav pointed to the wide wooden platform raised only a few centimetres off the ground. "That's what forklifts pick up." He continued inspecting the shed, avoiding looking Elsbeth in the eye. "This must be where they stored packing cases."

"At least the bathroom's still standing." Elsbeth pointed to a tiny building at the far end of the bombed-out factory. "There's no shower or bath. But we're lucky — there's a cold water tap. Jaroslav?" She stood directly in front of him. "Did you get the money?"

Emil piped up, "The owner of this place is Papa's friend. He lives in a villa." He started playing hop-scotch on the cement floor. "Anyway, we won't have to stay here long. Just until we find Mama and sail to Canada."

"I called at that villa. Herr Hoffer had said that's where you'd be staying. That place must have 50 rooms! Why couldn't we stay there?"

"Papa's friend is only allowed one large room and the kitchen in his own house. The State put so many strangers in all the other rooms that there wasn't room for us." Elsbeth sighed. "I don't care if I work till I drop, I'm going to get a villa just like his in Canada." Elsbeth was still planted in front of Jaroslav. "You didn't get the money, did you." It was more a statement than a question.

"You'd like to think I failed, wouldn't you? Leave me alone! My feet are swollen. I've been walking ever since I got off the train. I've got to talk to Herr Hoffer first." He threw himself down on the grey woolen blankets they'd brought with them from the American hospital. "We're going to get to Canada all right," he muttered.

He must have slept almost immediately because it was dark when he heard the big steel doors slide open. Elsbeth and Emil preceded Herr Hoffer into the shed.

"Welcome back, Jaroslav." Herr Hoffer shook his hand. "Did you get the money?"

Jaroslav avoided looking at the man as he swung his feet to the floor. "Sort of . . . I . . . I . . . hired a lawyer on your behalf."

Herr Hoffer's face turned as white as porcelain. "We need to talk about this, Jaroslav. Come, you and I, we will go to a café and drink a cup of coffee between us. Tell me all about it when we get there. Elsbeth, you and Emil climb into bed. We won't be gone long."

"No, Papa!" Elsbeth stood with her hands on her hips. "We all have a right to know if Jaroslav got the money. We need to know if we can go to Canada."

"All right, all right! I didn't get the money right now. But it's coming." Jaroslav blurted out the whole story. "I did the best I could. Herr Director wouldn't pay the bill, Herr Hoffer."

A long silence filled the shed. Finally Herr Hoffer said, "Come. We go for coffee now." As Emil started to smile, Herr Hoffer stood as erect as he could and added: "We are going to get to Canada, little ones. Nothing will stop us. Herr Director cheated us. But he will not defeat us. We just can't apply tomorrow as I hoped. But we will get there. You can count on it."

"It's okay, Papa." Emil took hold of his father's

hand. "It gives us more time to look around and see if Mama's here yet."

"She's not here!" Elsbeth sounded angry. But Emil ignored her as they set off.

That evening hadn't been so dreadful. Jaroslav ended up basking in being called "a brilliant strategist" by Herr Hoffer. Then one day drifted into the next, and before he was aware of it, the New Year had come and gone.

The real challenge was staying alive. Every day Jaroslav passed death on the street just outside their shed. A woman who had given up, a child too sick to fight for breath. Nuremberg had no shelter for the families that had lived there for centuries. Now the city was packed. Thousands of refugees camped in the refuse, owning only the tattered clothes on their backs.

But why are we different? Jaroslav wondered. It's this dream of going to Canada. That gives us something beyond just fighting to stay alive.

A couple of days later Herr Hoffer broke the thick depression that threatened to explode the shed. "I'm going to start my own business." He sounded thoughtful. "I should have thought of it earlier. I have friends from the Trade Association from before the war. They'll help me."

"The whole city is bombed out. How can you start a business, Papa?" Elsbeth sounded exasperated, but she watched her father carefully. Jaroslav realized that Elsbeth thought her father was going mad.

"Yesterday I heard the suburbs weren't bombed out. Two manufacturers are back in business." He began pacing back and forth, his enthusiasm boosting their spirits. "They've probably got out-dated machinery lying around unused in their sheds. I can persuade them to lend me some. I know I can." He flung his arm in a wide gesture. "Hoffer Incorporated. Elsbeth and Emil Hoffer, Directors; Jaroslav Jindrich, First Vice-President."

"How will that help us?" Jaroslav didn't even look around from where he was hanging up socks he had washed under the cold water tap. "We'll be on a treadmill. You'll have to pay big interest on the money you will have to borrow to buy the machinery. We'll never save enough money to get to Canada."

"Just shut up, Jaroslav." Elsbeth, spitting like an enraged cat, yanked his arm, sending socks flying everywhere. "My father has friends. Friends who owe him. What do you want us to do? Sit around here, mouthing English when we're not lining up for bread? We're all acting strange all the time. We've got to dig ourselves out of this refugee limbo. Right, Papa?"

"Right. Jaroslav, you ask around on the streets. See if you can find a man with a truck to haul the machinery. Find out if there are any cardboard mills operating. They can give us some on credit till we get into production." He began to brush off his suit and vest, and comb what was left of his hair.

"What are we going to make, Papa?" Emil looked up from where he was drawing a checkerboard on the cement floor.

"Paper boxes. Beautiful, lovely paper boxes. They can be traded for eggs and cheese and potatoes. Easter is coming. I can sell them to shipping companies. Canada, here we come." He buffed an old Homburg that he had found in the rubble of someone's house and plunked it on his head. Then he gave them a wave as he left the shed.

Everything came about exactly as Herr Hoffer had said. Except that Jaroslav was enraged when he saw the machinery. "When were these made? In the dinosaur age?" He stared at the ancient stitching and scoring machines, the cutting equipment and a machine to make crosses in cardboard.

"More like just after the Industrial Revolution," Herr Hoffer responded sarcastically. "What difference does it make, Jaroslav? They work." He strode over and grabbed hold of the boy by his shoulders. "We've got to fight to get out of here."

Weeks dragged by from the time Herr Hoffer filed application with the local authorities for permission to start up his factory. "What's the big problem?" Jaroslav asked one night as they all sat in a café eating watery soup with minute pieces of what they had been told was chicken.

"The authorities want entrepreneurs like me to give work to refugees. But everything is bombed out. There aren't any spaces for me to rent. They have to find spaces large enough that are still standing and requisition them. We'll just have to wait."

"Don't the owners get mad having their own places taken over by the State like that?" Elsbeth asked. "I would be furious. The Czech communists did that to you back home, Papa. Only they threw us into a camp. And you didn't like that!"

"No, I didn't. The owners here won't either. But they won't throw us into any camps, here in the Allied zone. But even here, the State has the right to interfere in people's lives when everything is in chaos. The State wants me to go into business. The State will help us."

"Toot-toot-to-toot-to-toot-too," Emil trumpeted through his fingers one day. "The Canadians are here, Papa! I saw lots of them stationed all around the Palace of Justice."

"What were you doing down there?"

"Looking for Mama, Elsbeth."

"Emil! I can't stand this! Mama's not here. She's in Russia." Her voice broke as she turned to Jaroslav. "We should go down and try to talk to these Canadians."

"What's going on, Herr Hoffer?" Jaroslav looked up from his phrase book. "For weeks, before these trials started, everyone was whispering. They shut up immediately if you asked them anything about it. Now the trials have finally started and the whole place is full of soldiers."

Herr Hoffer put down his pen. "You remember I told you something important in all of history was happening in Nuremberg?" As the children nodded, he continued. "The Nuremberg trials mean that high ranking officers will no longer be tried in the protection of a military court, but under common law as ordinary criminals, in front of judges from different countries."

Emil frowned. "What does that mean, Papa?"

"You remember how we were all packed off and sent to camps?" Herr Hoffer's eyes misted and he turned away. "Your mother was . . . you know . . . anyway, we suffered. We were starved, beaten, and some of your friends were tortured." His voice became hard. "We will never forget. This trial has declared that the people who did these things to us and to others can go to jail forever or be put to death as criminals."

There was a long silence, then Emil asked in a faint voice, "You mean that man who laughed when he shot all around Elsbeth's feet with a machine gun, when she was just trying to drink some water, will go to jail?"

Herr Hoffer sighed and crossed himself as Jaroslav felt the bitter taste of what had made Elsbeth so strong.

"That man is in Czechoslovakia," Herr Hoffer continued. "That's in the Russian zone. I don't know if Stalin, the head of Russia, will do the same thing. No one knows, although the Russians are here, taking part. The Nuremberg trials mean that if enough people testified that a man did that here in the Allied zone, he could be charged like any other ordinary criminal in a court of common law. He could not make the excuse that he was at war."

He jumped up and paced back and forth excitedly. "The Nuremberg trials will change history. From now on, a major or a sergeant can no longer commit an inhuman act and offer as an excuse that he was just following orders from the general. He will be held accountable for his own actions."

Wow! thought Jaroslav. All this has been going on and I didn't even know it. I want to see this. He made up his mind to go to the Palace of Justice the next morning.

But the next day Emil was shivering with fever and needed an egg, and Herr Hoffer heard of some cardboard way out to the west that had to be checked out. That day flowed into the next and the next and the next.

Abruptly, the economy went out of control in West Germany. Inflation began to creep, then walk, then streak through the country. Now Jaroslav paid eight marks for potatoes, which he could only find on the black market anyway, but next week he knew he would pay double, and the following month — if he could even find potatoes — five times as much. He watched in horror as the value of money dropped and the cost of passage to Canada soared.

Then unexpectedly — in the middle of his worry about money, as more and more shiny American jeeps, overflowing with tall, healthy soldiers, honked their way between twig-thin refugees picking a living out of dusty brick and crumbling mortar — Herr Hoffer was given space for his factory in an old tenement.

Anger choked Jaroslav in the morning and chilled him as he lay down at night. More work, he thought. My life is already nothing but work and sleep. If I'm extremely lucky, I eat. I don't sketch. I don't write. Forget school. If I didn't study by myself late at night before I pass out I'd never learn anything.

It shocked him that no one, himself included, had

spoken about Canada for weeks. Elsbeth and her father talked only about finding glue and stitching material. Emil was the only one who had branched out. He demanded English lessons, and Elsbeth took him to a woman who had once played piano concertos in England.

Jaroslav felt sick the day they moved to the suburbs. The ancient truck they borrowed heaved and creaked under the weight of all the machinery, and Jaroslav felt that Canada was waving goodbye forever to him.

That very morning he had noticed in his two-hour search for food that people were beginning to hoard.

"Fools," said Herr Hoffer when Jaroslav told him. "They think they'll keep an egg hidden for five days, then sell it for big money. They don't understand that during those five days, bread will have gone up so much that they have to turn around and spend five times as much to buy a loaf. They never get ahead."

As the truck lumbered its way through ancient mews to the inner buildings within a courtyard, Herr Hoffer gestured expansively. "Well, what do you think of it? See? We're down there." He pointed to the basement windows as Elsbeth dashed ahead into the tenement.

"We've got a toilet room and a little kitchen!" Chattering with excitement, Elsbeth brought them all running. "We've got a stove *and* a sink. Look, Emil, there's even a room for our family, next to the workshop."

Jaroslav saw that no sun would ever touch this factory workshop, and he felt miserable. The outer building, five stories high, would block out every beam of light. I've got to save myself, he almost moaned. Then he felt an arm around his shoulder.

"Next week, Jaroslav, after we're in production in the workshop, you find someone near the Palace of Justice who'll teach you — give you English lessons." Herr Hoffer said in a low voice, "Take a pretty paper box, our first, to pay for it."

"How did you . . . ?" Jaroslav stammered, flushing, then raced on. "I know I can find a Canadian to practise English on. I'll ask him about the trials. I'll ask him about Canada!"

Herr Hoffer nodded, smiling. "Exactly. In a month we will all sit down and figure out how long it will take us to get the passage money and apply for our visas to emigrate."

"Thank you, Herr Hoffer." For the first time Jaroslav reached for the older man and hugged him. As he was about to go up the steps leading to the outside to help unload machinery, he stopped. Turning, he said thoughtfully, "Maybe we all have it backwards, Herr Hoffer. Maybe we've always had it backwards. I think we should apply for our visas to emigrate first and worry about passage money later."

He was rewarded by seeing Herr Hoffer's eyes widen in appreciation of what he'd said. "As I said before, Jaroslav, you are a brilliant strategist. That is exactly what we will do. But first we have to get the factory started."

"Papa, we've got a new address now. We've got

to leave it for Mama." Emil was tugging at his father's sleeve.

"I'll send word back to the Americans in Bayreuth."

Elsbeth approached her father. "Papa, come outside. I have to talk to you." As soon as the door closed behind them, she turned on him. "Why are you lying to Emil? You know Mama's dead. If the work in the camp hasn't killed her, the Russian winter must have. Why don't you tell him the truth? I've had to accept it."

"He's too young for me to kill his dream."

"How's he going to feel when we don't find her? How's he going to feel when we sail without her to Canada? You didn't see how he disappeared inside himself just after they took Mama away. He could sink like that again."

"We'll cross that bridge when we get to it. Don't worry. By then he'll be old enough to handle it."

In the next month, glue, paper, wire and cloth were scrounged for the Hoffer factory in the little basement workshop. Two people showed up and begged for work, gambling that they might be paid in food. Elsbeth worked the stitching machine, Emil folded tiny boxes. Jaroslav would never have believed that boxes could look so delicate and lovely. He watched as Herr Hoffer finished hinging the first beautiful jewellery box.

"Can I take that?" he asked, reaching for it. "I think I know where I can sell it. I'm off now for my English lesson." He paused. "I might be a little late getting back."

Immediately after his lesson, he headed for the Palace of Justice. The first day he had gone for lessons he had spotted an older man at the far end, sitting outside, listening to classical music on the radio. Jaroslav had greeted him a few times. Today, he approached and after saying a few halting words in English, he asked what the man did.

"Civilian clerk. I work in the office of the captain. His regiment is on guard during these big trials. *Comprendez*?"

Jaroslav had listened carefully and nodded. He thought he understood. He drew the jewellery box out of an old paper bag. "You like?"

The man whistled. "Lovely," he said. "How much?"

Jaroslav was taken aback. He hadn't thought it would be so easy, and decided to ask a little more than it was worth in case he had to bargain. "Ten deutsch marks. Inflation." He paused. "Or two-fifty in American occupation money."

"Okay." The clerk counted out the money.

"Thank you." Jaroslav kissed the money and put it in his pocket carefully. "Bach — I like Bach, do you?"

The man smiled and nodded. "I used to write" — he made a scribbling gesture — "music column. Back home," he jerked with his thumb. "Cleveland, U.S.A."

Jaroslav nodded. "*Auf Wiedersehen*," he said, turning to go. Then he hesitated and turned back. "I bring four more. Tomorrow. Different. You have friends. They buy? *Ja?*"

The man grinned and clapped him on the back. "Any guy who likes Bach is okay. I'll ask around. See you later. *Comprendez?*"

Jaroslav made a plan, and two days later, pockets bulging with occupation money, he picked out an American soldier who looked trustworthy. He knew no one but American soldiers and their families were allowed inside their own grocery stores, called PXs. "Please," he said as he approached the soldier. "Here. Twenty-five dollars occupation money. Please. You buy fruit juice, chocolate bars and cigarettes for me? *Ja?*" Then he added quietly. "We are starving."

The American, who was only three years older than Jaroslav but who could have broken his body like a stick, couldn't look at him. "Yeah, okay, kiddo," he said, holding out his hand. "Gimme the dough. I'll be back in a jiff."

"That much for only twenty-five dollars?" Jaroslav's mouth dropped open when the soldier handed him a whole carton of chocolates, three cartons of cigarettes and several tins of fruit juice.

Later Jaroslav left one tin of fruit juice at home with Elsbeth and set off to peddle the rest in the black-market district.

"Don't be late," Elsbeth called after him. "Papa has a surprise for us. He left early this afternoon. He'll be back at nine o'clock."

At ten o'clock, Jaroslav returned, whistling a jaunty tune. One tin of apple juice had brought him twenty marks, the chocolates and cigarettes much more. Pockets bulging with money, he descended the steps leading to the factory and living quarters. He saw the candles burning in the family's room and wondered what surprise Herr Hoffer had brought home.

But when he opened the door, happy with his success, he found Herr Hoffer sitting dejectedly against the wall. Elsbeth had been crying and Emil had fallen asleep, his thumb in his mouth.

"What . . . ," he began.

"I went to the Canadian consul. No visas to emigrate are being issued. A German society in a Canadian city called Kitchener is organizing relief for the refugees in Germany. They are trying to bring over some refugees to Canada. But it's rumoured that they can bring in only five thousand from Germany." His voice broke. "Thousands have applied ahead of us."

13

A Treat and a Hope

*I*t was almost Christmas, over a year after their escape. They were still waiting for word from the lawyer in Hamburg that Herr Director would be forced to pay the money he owed Herr Hoffer.

Jaroslav was determined to celebrate this Christmas with something outstanding. And he knew just the thing. It's going to be tricky, he thought, but I know I can do it.

He sought out a public bathhouse, where he paid to hang his clothes in a tiny cubicle and walk naked to take his first shower in six months. Then he splurged, knowing the occasion demanded it, and bought the one-time use of a towel.

Smelling fresh and feeling revived, he boarded the train for the country to find a ham. A smoked ham is portable, he reasoned, and it'll last until Easter. The fact that I haven't seen or tasted a ham for two years doesn't matter. This Christmas Eve, we're going to eat ham!

He got off the train at a crossroads and asked at a few farmhouses — to no avail. He boarded a second train, travelled a bit farther, approaching farmhouse after farmhouse, still with no luck. As the sun began to set Jaroslav realized he'd travelled more than five hundred kilometres and still the only thing he had in his hands was another of the jewellery boxes he'd sold so easily to the clerk. He'd thought it would help him negotiate for the ham. But now he felt like throwing it in the ditch.

Thirsty and tired, he walked up a winding lane to what he had decided would be his last stop. "*Guten Abend*, Fräulein. Could I trouble you for a drink of water? I travelled too far." In search of a dream, he added to himself.

"Where are you from?" The woman tucked her wispy blonde hair under her hairnet.

"Nuremberg."

"Ah." Jaroslav felt her glance take in the dark circles under his eyes, his thin body. She went to the pump in the kitchen and returned with the water. "Things are bad in Nuremberg, I hear."

"*Ja*." Jaroslav thanked her and turned to go, hesitated, then held up the jewellery box. "I need to buy a ham. For Christmas. I might part with this as well to sweeten the deal."

Her hands, hummingbirds, whirred around the box. "Exquisite!" she breathed. Then still fingering the purple and silver paper dotted with exotic birds, she blurted, "I have a ham. I was saving it. Today it sells for 3,000 deutsch marks." She looked crafty. "I want the box too."

"I'll take it!" The words came out so quickly, the money changed hands so quickly, that the price didn't hit Jaroslav until he was walking down the road. Am I crazy to pay 3,000 marks for a ham? he wondered. Then his common sense took over. This is inflation, he thought. Yesterday the ham cost 2,500 marks. I came a day late. She's been hoarding all her good things. She thinks inflation will be over soon. Then she can sell her ham for "real money." No one, not even Jaroslav, considered the German mark to be "real money." It was so inflated it was almost useless.

That night, the ham clutched to his breast as he plodded home, Jaroslav's feet were so swollen that the most tender footstep on the dirt road made him wince. He barely caught the train. I should be glad I can surprise everyone, he thought. So why am I so depressed?

His eyelids were heavy, but he was afraid to sleep in case his ham was stolen. No one else was carrying a round lump, obviously meat, wrapped in newspaper.

Jaroslav tried to conjure up his own father's face. But the memory of the Jindrich mouth and eyes was fading. He felt a stab of fear and knew he had to change his life. No one's going to do it for me, he said. It's up to me.

Saying many Hail Marys for getting his ham safely back to Nuremberg, Jaroslav made an important decision as he picked his way back to the Hoffers' home.

"A room of my own," he said aloud, then whirled, scared by a sudden sound behind him. But the December moon spilled silver over the tenement, and Jaroslav stopped to look up at it. Perhaps he could find his own room right here. He could keep a journal of what was happening all around him. Maybe he could decorate the walls with his drawings.

"A ham!" Elsbeth screamed three weeks later, on Christmas Eve, as a grinning Jaroslav held out the smoked meat. "Oh, Jaroslav!" She threw her arms around him, then backed away, suddenly embarrassed.

"Give me a piece, right now." Emil, cheeks flushed, hurled himself at Jaroslav.

Later, on their way home from Midnight Mass, Jaroslav told the family of his decision.

Herr Hoffer's dismay was obvious. "But why are you leaving us? It's important we all stay together. I promised your father." Opening the door, he reached for the ham again, tears in his eyes. "A ham, a real ham."

"I'm not going very far. After all, I'm sixteen now." Jaroslav smiled. "I found a garret up on the fifth floor. A woman and her son are moving to Hamburg after New Year's. I paid her some extra marks to rent her room to me. Anyway, Merry Christmas, Herr Hoffer. Remember, though, I'm still the First Vice-President of Hoffer Incorporated."

First they all took turns smelling the ham. Then they unwrapped it and smelled it again. They cut thin slices and nibbled, savouring the rich smoky taste.

"Remember mama's homemade mustard?" Elsbeth asked.

Emil's colour seemed to heighten as he bit into the first meat he'd had in four months. "Where's our good-luck guest?" he asked. "Remember, Papa? Mama always invited one. If we have a good-luck guest, Mama is sure to find us."

Herr Hoffer nodded, reflected for a moment, then snapped his fingers. "Jaroslav, walk over and bring back your English teacher. We don't have a piano, but you said she sometimes plays. Maybe she'll hum some Strauss waltzes for us." He paused. "If this helps Mama wherever she is, so much the better."

An hour later, Fräulein Elten, complete with lorgnette and cigarette holder, entered the family room. She wrinkled her nose. "Ham," she said. "I must be dreaming. I smell smoked ham."

Jaroslav laughed. "You're our good-luck guest for Christmas. Here, please have a piece."

The ham was snatched out of his hands almost as soon as he cut it. Fräulein Elten wolfed it down. Suddenly embarrassed, she mumbled, "I haven't had meat since I arrived in Nuremberg." She couldn't take her eyes off the ham.

Jaroslav cut another, thicker slice, and she ate it more slowly. Then she looked up at them. "What is it you want from me?"

"Papa said you'd hum Strauss waltzes for us for Christmas," Emil said. He was showing her his one and only present — a maze made of cardboard, covered with green and brown paper.

"You're joking, *ja?*" she asked wearily. "You want something from me. No one gives a piece of meat without wanting something bigger than a Strauss waltz."

Herr Hoffer stepped forward, bowed and raised her hands to his lips. "I greet you as an artist, Fräulein Elten. What could be more important than Strauss waltzes on Christmas Eve? Let us begin." With that he encircled her waist and began to whirl her around the small room. Before the first twirl, her throaty contralto voice had begun to fill the room. Soon, all of them were singing and dancing as they greeted the first minutes of Christmas Day, 1947.

Bells coated with hoarfrost were ringing in the dawn of Christmas Day when Fräulein Elten finally left. She paused a moment in the doorway.

"Since before the war I have not eaten so well or had so much fun. I have watched you, Jaroslav, doodling on paper when I kept you waiting. I think you have a talent for sketching. I could teach you the technique." She held up her hand to cut off any protests. "No charge. You already pay me for the English lessons. That is enough. Can you get hold of a drawing pad and pencils for next time? We always make room for a budding artist." She sighed. "My brother, God rest his soul, could draw and paint like Michelangelo. He showed me a little, now I will show you. And now, thank you all again for the best Christmas I've had since before the war."

The honey wagon arrived to pump the excrement out of the tenement septic tanks the day Jaroslav moved. Not even the wretched stench that rose right up to his garret room dampened his spirits. For the first time he felt a real sense of freedom.

His room barely had space for a bed, table and bookshelf, and he had the use of a shared free-fall toilet down the hall — one that didn't use running water. There was a basin with a cold water tap on each floor where he could wash himself. His life-style hadn't improved, but he was as happy as a rabbit in a cabbage patch. And he hung up his first pieces of art — sketches of faces and people done either out on the street or from Fräulein Elten's window.

"The Americans have set up their own library, I just heard." Elsbeth had come in to visit Jaroslav and see what his room looked like. "They're using the books they brought over for the army to read. It's in the basement next to the Palace of Justice. Oh, listen, I almost forgot. Papa wants us to continue to eat together, okay? We've got to talk. About that list for Canada."

"Libraries take too much time," Jaroslav said. "By the time the librarian has given you the third degree and made you sign in blood for a card, it isn't worth it." Jaroslav had a pin in his mouth. He was sticking up his latest drawings. "I only ate by myself the last few days for the heck of it."

"Listen, Jaroslav, the Americans have got super new pocket books. They're not old and dusty like the ones the German libraries have. And they don't send the police after you if you don't bring the books back on time." Elsbeth's head was tilted as she examined Jaroslav's sketches. "Not bad."

"Have you been there?"

"No. I'm back at school now. By the time I've done a couple of hours of work in the factory, the day's gone. But I can hardly wait to read some of their books. They're all in English. I can practise."

The moment she left, Jaroslav raced down the stairs and through the streets to the American library. He approached the librarian, who was sitting reading with his feet up on the desk.

"Hey buddy, how're ya doin'?" the librarian greeted Jaroslav, who had begun to bow to him in traditional German deference to a librarian.

"I would like to read. I do not have a card." He held up his briefcase. "I can have two books, *ja?*" Jaroslav knew that German libraries limited the number of books withdrawn.

"Ya gotta have a card," said the librarian, smiling. "Gimme your name and approximate address." He filled one out and handed it to Jaroslav. "Help yourself." He gestured towards the metal shelves.

"But, sir, only librarians can go in there. I cannot go in there. I wish two books. Any two books."

"Look, man, I got important reading here myself. Go on back." He gestured with his arm. "Pick out your own books." Jaroslav could hardly believe it when the man added, "Take home as many as you like. Only two hard, fast rules. You gotta use your card every time you take books out. And you gotta bring the books back in three weeks. Is that enough time? If not, drop by. We'll renew them."

Jaroslav stood for a moment, his mouth open. Then he nodded, grinning, and walked to the stacks. As he meandered between the shelves he struggled to read the beginnings of these books written in a strange tongue. Finally Steinbeck, Hemingway and Dos Passos were packed into his briefcase like words into a dictionary. Sure, these are all by American writers, Jaroslav figured, but they can still tell me what a super life we're going to have in Canada. It's not that different.

Back home, struggling to decipher the new language, he was stunned. He was reading about North Americans who were not rich but poor and starving and whose spirits had been broken way back in the 1930s.

Jaroslav threw the first book down. He stared out the window for a long time. They're just like me here in Germany in 1947, he thought. An icicle of fear made him shiver. Maybe going to Canada's a bad move. He shook himself, hard. Come on, Jaroslav, nothing could be worse than staying here. But Canada's not going to be easy. I bet there's no black market to make money on over there.

Within a few months, by concentrating on his reading, Jaroslav was able to understand and read English almost perfectly. But he still spoke haltingly, with an accent. But I'm ready now, he thought. At least in Canada there'll be some older people who lived through the Depression. They'll understand how hard we had to work to get over there.

The library had become so popular with the Germans as well as all the refugees that it had moved to what had been the Turkish Consulate. The Americans now stocked it with the latest hard-cover books.

"You're our best customer," the librarian said. "But I gotta admit, that sister of yours runs a close second." Jaroslav just smiled.

He and Elsbeth would sit up past midnight arguing about what life in Canada would be like. "At first I was depressed when I read these." Jaroslav had gestured towards a pile on his desk. "But the characters in these books trust each other. They're open with each other. The writers tell it like it was." He sighed, turning away from her. "Who's going to do that for us?"

"That's only in books, Jaroslav. Sure it's different here. No one trusts anyone. We all wish we were back home in our own countries. I watch what I say outside the family. And you, you're lucky if you have half an hour to write. Just to find a potato for supper takes us two days. Anyway, what's all this got to do with Canada?"

"It gives me hope. Maybe Canadians are like Americans. Maybe they're more open because it's such a huge country. Hardly anyone lives in most of it." Jaroslav crossed his arms and leaned against the window sill. "Anyway, you wouldn't be taking time off from homework if you didn't think reading these books would help *you* in Canada."

"I'm learning English just like you are." Elsbeth shifted to get a cramp out of her leg. "Just because one character in some American book you've read says Canada's huge and has lots of factories and some railroads and he's thinking of going there, doesn't mean it's true." She sighed. "People think we're strange because we want to go to Canada. Everyone's dream here is to go to America. Who knows anything for sure about Canada? There are no books from there."

"Yeah, but there's food there, Elsbeth. Remember that American back at the hospital who put his cigarette out in the butter? No one here would ever do that even when we were growing up. All the people in Europe are squashed tight into tiny countries. We were lucky if we qualified to advance in school. Our parents were lucky if they could make a go of some little business or a farm, because then we could eat well. Who has butter on bread here? We use chicken fat."

Elsbeth nodded. "You're right, Jaroslav. Canadian soldiers throw half their food in the garbage — lucky for us. Even some of those civilians who were here for the trials were fat. Here in Europe, if you're fat it means you're rich."

"Exactly." Jaroslav shook his finger for emphasis.

"So we'll be okay because there's lots of food over there. As long as we can eat, we can work." She paused for a moment, frowning. "I wish we could read some books written by Canadians, though."

"The soldiers I spoke to said it wasn't all that different from America. One Canadian warned me to tell everyone we were from Czechoslovakia and not from Germany. Canadians think everyone who comes in from Germany is the enemy."

Elsbeth jumped up, a caged wildcat, pacing. "Are Canadians so stupid they think because we come in on a visa from Germany that we're Germans? Are they so stupid they think all Germans are bad? Don't they know anything about what's happened over here?" She gestured wildly. "We need someone to tell our story."

Jaroslav had given lots of thought to what she'd said. He'd also been sketching as much as he'd been reading. Some refugees posed for him. "Maybe I'll go down in history," one old man had said, twirling his handlebar moustache. And inspired by all his reading and sketching, a wild dream took root in Jaroslav's heart.

"Papa's heard a rumour, Jaroslav." Elsbeth burst into his room late one evening. "The Canadian government is about to take independent action. Something about passing orders in council. Papa says that might mean we can all go to Canada right away."

Jaroslav had been hanging up a sketch of a gaunt refugee woman holding out three oranges, but he caught the excitement in Elsbeth's voice and left the picture dangling at an angle. "This is a sign. A real sign. Now I know I've made the right career decision for Canada."

"Papa has to go to Munich on business. He wants you to go to the Canadian Consulate this week. You've got to find out what this means for us." She walked over to look at his latest drawings. "What do you mean, *career decision?*" she mocked. "You're going to work for Papa, aren't you?"

"There's food for the picking there, Elsbeth." Jaroslav was so excited he could hardly stand still. "People can hop on board a train that takes them thousands of kilometres and they don't even leave their own country. They don't have to show a passport. They don't get thrown in jail. The police there are gentle compared to police here in Europe. They even have a word for themselves when they ride the rails. They call themselves hobos." He flung his arms wide, smiling. "I want to be one!"

"Are you crazy, Jaroslav?" Elsbeth frowned. "What about getting money to bring your own father over to Canada?"

They stared at each other, each knowing that Jaroslav's father would never be allowed to leave. Jaroslav turned away. "I'll do whatever I have to do," he muttered. "Look, Elsbeth, I'd be free. I could wander across an empty country. I wouldn't see one bombed-out city. Think of it." He reached for his pad. "I'm going to be a hobo. I'm going to sketch other D.P.s who went to Canada like us. I'm going to write our stories. I don't — "

He stopped when he noticed the expression on Elsbeth's face. She had taken down the sketch of the "orange lady" and was staring at it, turning it first this way and then that.

"It can't be . . . " she whimpered, throwing the sketch on the bed. She tried to turn away, but fascinated by the face, she held up the sketch again. "Mama's dead. I've told Emil over and over. Mama's dead." She threw it down again and ran from the room, leaving the door gaping behind her.

Jaroslav had just picked up his picture to look at it, when he heard Elsbeth's quavering voice in the doorway. "Where did you find this woman?"

"By the Palace of Justice."

"It looks like Mama." Her voice was so low Jaroslav had to strain to hear her. He stared at her and wondered if she was finally having a breakdown. She's been working too hard since we arrived, he thought. She's never let up, not even with going to school. She's finally broken. Aloud he said, "Elsbeth, I met your mother, once back home. Don't you think I — "

"Emil was right. Mama could be alive." She rushed out again. "Come on, Jaroslav. We've got to get Papa and go and find her."

Herr Hoffer took the sketch over to the window. "I don't know. With that babushka — it might be — but it's only a sketch." He cleared his throat. "It can't be. No one gets away from a labour camp. Jaroslav, you and I will go down to the Palace of Justice. Elsbeth, you stay here with Emil."

"No, I'm coming too."

"I knew Mama was here." Emil was already halfway out the door.

The streets were dark and cluttered. The military police were patrolling in jeeps through streets that had now been cleared of rubble, trying to spot some black marketeers. It was about ten kilometres to the Palace of Justice, and Emil, riding on Jaroslav's shoulders, was nodding off when at last they arrived.

"She was sitting right here," Jaroslav said.

Elsbeth pointed to a guard chewing gum and reading a comic book. "Papa, ask him if he knows where the lady with the oranges lives."

"Sorry, Pops. She sells her oranges and then goes. Ya gotta come back in coupla days. She'll be back then." He went back to Batman. "Hey," he called after them. "She don't look too good." He made a circular motion with his finger at his temple. "Sometimes she talks crazy, ya know what I mean? Hope ya find 'er."

That night, it wasn't just the summer heat steaming the eaves above Jaroslav's tiny room that kept him awake. It was that Frau Hoffer hadn't recognized him and he hadn't recognized her.

It can't be her, he told himself. She can't have changed so much. And nobody escapes from a Russian labour camp. But in his heart he knew he was wrong. Prisoners did escape. He fell asleep seeing the soldier twirling his finger at his temple.

14

Together

*E*lsbeth scratched her face too hard, leaving splotches of red. Emil was curled up on what was left of a small wall, sleeping. Jaroslav, who had gone with them, lounged against a post, reading. He had become bored — the Nuremberg trials were over — watching the salutes and shouldering of rifles that marked what was left of the military coming and going from the Palace of Justice.

The three of them had been keeping watch every day, in spite of what the soldier had said. "The woman might turn up if she runs out of money. We've got to go and find out who she is, Papa." Elsbeth dressed warmly, pocketed their last share of the ham and darted off. She had prowled up and down the street so often that Jaroslav was relieved today when she turned to him and said, "The dead don't walk up to you carrying oranges. We all know that." Then she yawned.

Jaroslav was caught in a quandary. He knew soon he would have to go looking for food. But he couldn't leave Elsbeth and Emil alone. And Herr Hoffer had to run the factory.

Oh, Herr Hoffer told him that he himself had managed to get two potatoes and some bread, but he looked haggard from overwork and worry. The only word from the Hamburg lawyer, except for the first of many bills, was that Herr Director had registered the debt with the Allied Commission for repatriation of the money. He had washed his hands of the debt. "We must establish the validity of the amount owing and as you know I made application to apply before the tribunal," the lawyer wrote. "Our suit is currently being considered by yet another commission. We will just have to wait."

"Damn!" Herr Hoffer had said when he read the letter. "Because Germany lost the war, all of us in the countries Germany conquered have lost control of our affairs. The courts are treating us like children, making decisions for us about our own businesses. *We're* not war criminals. We're just people struggling to get our businesses back on track."

"Can I look at your book?" Elsbeth yawned again and held out her hand. She began reading, mouthing the English words, and Jaroslav sat down beside her. He closed his eyes and leaned back. He wondered if the "orange lady" — he refused to think of her as Frau Hoffer — would ever show up.

Jaroslav heard the shuffling before Elsbeth did.

"Oranges?" a voice murmured tentatively, a little distance away, as a woman, thin even in three layers of sweaters, held out two of the fruits to passers-by. Her boots were made of double-woven straw, the kind usually worn indoors only. She wore a faded print skirt above mended sagging stockings.

Her hunched body and yellow complexion made her look old under the babushka, made Elsbeth hesitate, unsure, as she bent to quietly waken Emil.

"Wait." Jaroslav put his hand on her arm. "Let her get closer." The sound of straw scraping against cobblestones grew louder. Urgently, Jaroslav whispered, "If it's your mother, she'll know you."

The woman was almost upon them. Glancing at Jaroslav, she had just murmured, "Ah, the artist," when all the pain and disbelief boxed up inside Elsbeth pushed the girl towards this stranger.

"Who are you? Why are you here?" she cried, grabbing the "orange lady." The woman, frightened, stumbled backwards.

Face to face with her, Elsbeth froze. "Mama?" Her voice caught, then a tear ran slowly down her cheek. "It is you, Mama. I didn't know you!" They stood staring at each other until, sobbing, Elsbeth tried to put her arms around the woman. "Mama, I've missed you so much. I thought you were dead. How can you be alive? How can you be here?" She was crying so loudly that Emil sat up, rubbing his eyes.

"Mama!" he yelled, jumping to his feet. "I knew you were in Nuremberg. I kept telling them." He hurled himself towards both of them.

Struggling not to fall, the woman tried to push

the children away. "Let me go! Help! Help! You! Artist! Help me, for God's sake help me." Her knees buckled and she fell, crying.

"Jaroslav, get some water from that soldier." Elsbeth knelt and gathered the woman in her arms. "Jaroslav came with us, remember? Please remember, Mama." She buried her head in her mother's neck, crying.

"Here, kid, take the canteen." The soldier held it out. "I don't speak German, but them kids should back off. The old dame's crazy, you know what I mean? She's probably hungry too. Hardly anybody gets oranges over here except us Americans. Why she don't eat her damn oranges, I don't know. She's always sellin' 'em instead of eatin' 'em."

As he took the canteen, Jaroslav cursed the soldier for not knowing that selling the rare oranges had kept a safe roof over the woman's head, which was more important in bombed-out Nuremberg than eating them up. "She's lucky one of your soldiers buys oranges at your PX for her to sell," he snapped, and hurried back to Elsbeth.

"Drink, Mama." Elsbeth handed the woman the canteen. "Please, listen to me. We had our passports. You gave them to me, remember?"

The woman shoved the canteen aside and struggled to her knees. "Leave me alone," she cried, tears falling down her cheeks. "You can't be Elsbeth. Elsbeth was just a child. She would never last outside the camp without me."

"But we did, Mama. I had the money, remember? I met Jaroslav outside the camp. We were brave. We made our way over the mountains. It took weeks. We crossed No Man's Land to freedom."

Giggling, then laughing wildly, the "orange lady" got to her feet. "You're lying to me. Why are you doing this?" Elsbeth shrank back. "Leave me alone. You're cruel." She wiped her face. As she moved away she tripped and almost fell. "I had an Elsbeth," she whispered. "You have Elsbeth's hair. She had your eyes. I had an Els . . . "

Emil, who had fallen back to watch, came up beside the "orange lady." He gently took her hand in his and began stroking it. "Tell me a story, Mama. About the man with the blue beard? Please, Mama. Remember? Please come home now." He started towards home, tugging her. "Come on, Mama. I need to hear my story."

"Emil?" The word was spoken with awe. "Elsbeth? No. No, it can't be." She kept shaking her head, as if to clear it. "I don't believe it. It can't be."

Dazed, Frau Hoffer gave in and stumbled after her son. The four of them stopped many times to rest. Jaroslav persuaded her to eat one of the oranges and the children shared the other. "We have a bit of food at home," he explained. "Herr Hoffer has started a little factory in a basement workroom. It makes paper boxes and it also makes a little money. The Hoffers live behind the factory."

When they reached the door of the tenement, Emil pulled his mother down the stairs. But she began to panic, turning wildly from side to side as she pulled away and tried to run back up the stairs.

The door at the bottom opened. "Hildegarde. Oh,

my Hildegarde," he said quietly. Herr Hoffer stepped forward and gathered the woman into his arms. "I didn't dare believe you might be alive." His voice broke. "We are together, at last."

Frau Hoffer alternated between weeping and laughing. She kept running her hands over their faces, examining their noses, tweaking their ears, holding up Elsbeth's hair, hugging Emil, until at length she collapsed, exhausted.

Herr Hoffer offered her his last piece of ham. Wide-eyed at the miracle of a piece of ham, she wolfed it down. Then her eyes, drooping, finally closed, and she fell asleep.

"But she didn't tell us what happened to her," pouted Emil. "That soldier said she was crazy. *He's* crazy."

"Tomorrow," Herr Hoffer said, finger to his lips to quiet him. "Mama will tell us all about it tomorrow."

Jaroslav sat in a corner of the room, watching. He felt more and more alone. This woman didn't seem crazy to him. She acted just like a lot of single frightened refugee women who were alone, who didn't get enough to eat.

What am I going to do now? he wondered, feeling wretched. Now that Frau Hoffer was back, the Hoffers were again together as a family, and he, Jaroslav, was an outsider. I wish my father would turn up just like Frau Hoffer. He immediately stifled the wish, because he knew it would never come true.

Abruptly he said goodnight and climbed the five flights to his garret room. There he remembered

Elsbeth dashing in and telling him about the orders in council. I'll go there tomorrow morning, first thing, he thought. If I can write and sketch in a country where there's lots to eat, I won't feel so left out.

He fell asleep almost remembering his own father's eyes.

The next day, while Herr Hoffer kept watch over his wife, who opened her eyes once, smiled, then fell asleep again, Jaroslav went to the Canadian Consulate to apply for their visas. This time he would add Frau Hoffer's name to the list.

"Have you been here before?" the secretary asked him, smiling.

"No. I've come for the forms for the Hoffer family."

"I think I remember the Hoffers' names on the list. Are you the older brother?" She smiled again and began flirting a little with him as she got out the forms.

"Not exactly . . . uh . . . I'm a . . . cousin." He knew she didn't believe him, but he kept looking at the forms. "These look straightforward enough."

"It's more complicated than you think. Getting to Canada, I mean." The girl combed her hair and pulled at her skirt.

"Complicated?"

"You have to be needed in Canada. You have to be working at one of the occupations they prefer." Her eyes seemed locked on Jaroslav's. "And forget it if you're not related to the family. You can't get visas together. You'd have to apply alone."

Jaroslav ignored her remark about not being related. "There must be a list somewhere. Of preferred occupations, I mean." He smiled at her.

"Sure. Right here in my desk. But it's confidential. Very confidential." She stared at him, then suddenly stood up. "Be back in ten minutes." She pulled one drawer half open, winked and said, "I live in Halifax if you ever get across the ocean."

Jaroslav waited till she had turned the corner, then yanked the drawer wide open. Quickly he wrote down the first ten preferred occupations. Engineer is the second, he read. Herr Hoffer could call himself an engineer after all the things he's done.

Then he saw another notation: "Eastern Canada heavily populated. Preference will be given to immigrants who desire to go to the furthest ends of Canada, e.g., British Columbia." He wrote Vancouver on his list. I'll say we're going to Vancouver, he decided.

He closed the drawer just as the girl returned. "You need to produce a letter of recommendation," she said. "You're a student? Get a letter stating you're an honour student. Get them to write that you'd be a great salesman."

Jaroslav's confusion showed.

"The government analyzes newspaper ads across Canada in the different cities. Then they put them all into categories. There's more ads for salesmen than for anything else. Engineers come a close second." She winked again. "My name's Margot O'Reilly if you ever stop over in Halifax.

Look me up. Who knows, I could be home on leave."

Jaroslav smiled and wrote down her name. "Canada will be wonderful, Margot O'Reilly," he said. "Have you heard of hobos? I want to be one and ride on the trains. I'm going to write what happened to all us D.P.s."

"Oh no! Don't tell them that. Put down you're going to be a salesman." She frowned. "And listen, you've got a real problem if you're not part of the family. Your visas could come through at different times. Or yours could come through and theirs might not. Or vice versa. Think about it."

Jaroslav waved as he left. But he was worried. It looks like I'm a real outsider now, he thought. Even my passport could come through at a different time. If I go over by myself to Canada I might never find the Hoffers. I . . . I . . .

He fought to control his panic. Things are looking better, he told himself. I have the information at least. I have the forms. I just have to talk to Herr Hoffer and bring them back, filled out. In spite of his pep talk to himself, he felt worry block his way at every corner on the walk home.

"Splendid, Jaroslav." Herr Hoffer beamed at him when he produced the forms. "Now we need letters of recommendation. I can get mine from business friends here in Germany. Then we need a clean bill of health from the doctor for all of us."

"I have to apply separately." Jaroslav tried to say it lightly as if it didn't matter very much.

"Why separately?"

"I'm not part of the family."

Herr Hoffer understood right away. "Then your visa could come through at a different time." He began to pace back and forth. "If we can't go together, we don't go."

"You can't stay here because of me. You have to get out as soon as you can." Jaroslav felt his voice rise in hysteria. "We've all got to get away from this nightmare."

"Let me think. Go out and see if you can find a little real coffee to bring back for Hildegarde. She's still sleeping. I'm worried. I hope she isn't sick."

Miserable, and almost feeling ill himself, Jaroslav left. He knew he had to go to the inner city to get real coffee, and suddenly he had an idea. I could type up my own letter of recommendation on the stationary of an optical company Herr Hoffer supplies with paper boxes, he thought.

When he had finished his one-finger picking at the typewriter in the outer office, he went in to see the manager. "Will you sign this? It says I'm a great salesman and an honour student."

"Of course, Jaroslav." The manager signed instantly. "Canada doesn't know you yet, but it won't be long before they do. Don't worry. You'll do well there." Then he frowned. "You'll have to work hard and be a good salesman in Canada. There's lots of unemployment, I hear."

Jaroslav, whose spirits had begun to rise, was startled. He had never thought there might be people out of work in the land of opportunity. The Great Depression was long over.

"Just stick to your story about being a salesman. You'll be okay."

Jaroslav then went to a company that made wooden toys and typed up another letter. Feeling a bit better, he took the letters and coffee home.

"I've got the answer, Jaroslav." Herr Hoffer almost yanked him through the door as soon as he arrived. "I've thought it over carefully. I want you to be legally part of our family. I know Hildegarde will agree with me."

Jaroslav wondered what the man was talking about and wished Herr Hoffer would get to the point.

"In a way, you already are part of our family." Herr Hoffer paced back and forth, the coffee for his wife forgotten. "You were my emissary to Herr Director in Hamburg, just like a son. You helped me start the factory here, just like a son. You brought us the ham, just like a son. In fact, Jaroslav" — Herr Hoffer swung around and faced him — "*you will be our son*. We wish to adopt you."

Jaroslav stared at Herr Hoffer. "Sorry, I can't do that," he said slowly. He turned to go to his garret. "I have my own father."

15

Something to Celebrate

Jaroslav stretched out on his bed. Guilt lay thick and heavy across him as he stared at the ceiling, unable to sleep that night. He had finally got away from Herr Hoffer. "You can't say no, Jaroslav. It's our only chance to get out of here together," he had kept calling up the stairs.

Why couldn't Herr Hoffer understand? Of all of them, his dream of going to Canada was the brightest. He spoke English perfectly. He had saved his own money from sales on the black market. Above all, he knew exactly what he was going to do in Canada. He burned with desire to talk to other D.P.s in a new land and write and sketch about it. He loved the word *hobo*. It made him feel free of this dusty flattened country. "Hobo, hobo, hobo."

There was a soft knock at his door. Jaroslav held his breath. Go away, he thought. Go away. But the knocking persisted. With a huff, he opened the door.

"Jaroslav, we must talk." Herr Hoffer had brought some hot coffee with him. "Please let me come in."

Jaroslav nodded and stepped aside. "I can't be your son," he muttered. "Go ahead to Canada without me. I'll get there later, on my own."

"Listen, Jaroslav." Herr Hoffer put his hand on the boy's shoulder. "I know you feel guilty. If you agree to be adopted by us, it's as if you want your own father to be dead. Isn't that it?"

Jaroslav slumped onto the edge of his bed, his head in his hands. "Yes," he said.

"Your father risked being sent to a labour camp in Russia when he gave us money and passports in the first place. If your father hadn't been determined to get you out of Czechoslovakia, we would still be sitting back in the camps in Saaz. I made your father a promise. I would take you to Canada with us."

"No adoption, Herr Hoffer. It would hurt my father too much." He clenched his fists at his temples. "I can't do it."

Minute stretched into minute while Herr Hoffer sipped his coffee. At length he leaned towards Jaroslav. "It's just a piece of paper. It's just to get what your father wants for you. We all respect your father. Lots of refugee families have to adopt to get a survivor out with them." He took a deep breath. "Right now it's quick and it's easy. Germany wants these refugees to move on to any other country."

He put down his cup. "Once we get to Canada, you'll write to your father — or I can send word through my business friends who go across the border — that you're safe. We'll forget about the adoption once we're across the ocean. Once we're safe." Herr Hoffer watched Jaroslav closely.

"But what if my father should find out from your business friends what I've done? He would be so hurt."

"Your father is worried sick about you, Jaroslav. He wants you to get as far away from the KGB as you can." He paused. "It's just a piece of paper. He won't be hurt. He'll be relieved that his son, whom he loves, is safe, the same way I would be if Emil was in your place."

The two sat silently, thinking. Jaroslav got up and looked out his window down at the mews. "Do you think I could get word to him that I made it to Canada?"

"I'm sure of it." Herr Hoffer looked happy again. "Once we get our passage booked, I'll try to let him know, even before we leave to take the train to Hamburg."

"He'll be relieved?" Jaroslav looked at Herr Hoffer. "You think he'll understand?"

"You know, Jaroslav, your father's smart. He's smart enough to be a commissar. He's probably figured out already what we have to do to get across the ocean to Canada. He'll be happy we've solved the problem of staying together."

"All right, I'll do it." Immediately Jaroslav smiled. He had been hungry to get to Canada, but he hadn't dared admit that he was scared to go alone. And everything Herr Hoffer had said was true. In Canada he'd save his money, then come back to try to bring his real father out of Czechoslovakia.

Herr Hoffer hugged him. "Remember when I called you a brilliant strategist? Well, this is just a strategy for getting us to Canada. I'll get the papers and make arrangements tomorrow. Then we can fill out the visa forms."

Jaroslav opened his door. "Thanks, Herr Hoffer." He hesitated, then added quickly. "You have been like a father to me . . . "

"Say no more, Jaroslav. It's settled." The older man stepped into the hall. "Oh, by the way, Elsbeth said a priest was looking for you. He left an address on a piece of paper and asked that you call on him."

A priest, Jaroslav thought, climbing into bed. I wonder what a priest could want?

The next day he was relieved to see that no one made any fuss over his decision. Frau Hoffer was smiling as she lay in bed, flanked by Elsbeth and Emil.

"We're taking the day off school to be with Mama." Elsbeth's face was radiant. "Tonight she's going to tell us how she got here. Aren't you, Mama?"

"Yes, *liebchen*." Frau Hoffer looked up at Jaroslav. "You've grown. Your father would be proud to see how tall you are now."

"A priest was looking for you, Jaroslav," Emil piped up, wiggling off the bed. "Can I go with you if you go and see him?"

"Sure. What rectory is it?"

"He's staying at a first-class hotel." Elsbeth seemed impressed as she gave Jaroslav the address.

"A hotel? Did he speak with a Czech accent?" he asked, suddenly anxious about his father.

"Not that I could hear."

Jaroslav took Emil's hand and they set off. No sooner were they around the corner and out of sight when Jaroslav stopped. "Your Mama's back. We should find something special to eat tonight, to celebrate. What do you think?"

"We can't afford another ham. What can we get, Jaroslav?"

"Noodles."

"Noodles? There aren't any noodles in Nuremberg!"

"We don't know that until we try. Come on. Let's go."

"But what about the priest?"

"Forget the priest. I'll see him later. Any priest who's staying at a first-class hotel is having a good time. He won't be in any rush to leave. Let's get the noodles."

Three hours later, Emil's feet dragged and his mouth drooped as Jaroslav was still asking this woman with the cart on the street, that man behind a counter in a store, that girl selling a chocolate bar. No noodles in all of Nuremberg.

"Come on, Emil. We need some coffee." He hoisted the boy onto his shoulder and carried him into a tiny café sprouting out of the rubble. "*Guten Tag*," Jaroslav called as he lowered Emil onto a chair.

"*Ja?*" The owner smiled at the two of them.

"Coffee, please. Just one, we'll share it." Jaroslav handed her the money. His feet hurt and he was angry that he had failed in his search for noodles.

"You live here in Nuremberg, *ja?*" The woman

put down the cup of steamed chicory, terrible tasting, that passed for coffee. "You do sketching. I've seen you, *ja?*"

"*Ja,*" Jaroslav said wearily. "Today I'm not sketching. Today I'm looking for noodles."

"Mama escaped from a Russian labour camp. She's home with us now. Jaroslav promised to bring back noodles." Emil's head was propped up on his elbow, resting against the table. He yawned. "But we couldn't find any."

"Noodles, eh?" The woman suddenly became businesslike. "Noodles are expensive." She looked all around to see if anyone was watching. "Of course, it's not every day a woman stays alive walking from Russia to Germany. Wait. I will be right back." Five minutes later she held out a transparent cellophane package of green noodles. "One hundred marks. Do you want them? Hurry up."

Jaroslav thanked her and quickly paid her the marks. Emil, wide awake now, turned the package over and over in his hands. "Why are they green, Jaroslav?"

"They're spinach noodles. We'll get more vitamins from them. Tuck them under your jacket, Emil. We must go."

"I want to go home and cook them right now."

"It's a long walk to get home. I haven't any money left for a bus. It's lunch time, so why don't we go and see the priest now. His hotel is right around the corner. Maybe he'll offer us some soup or something."

There was only one priest in the hotel lobby, and he was a monsignor, distinctive in his red and black garb, sitting smoking a cigar and reading a news-paper.

Jaroslav was astounded as he greeted the priest. He'd never seen such a mammoth man. The monsignor looked to be nearly seven feet tall.

"He's fat," whispered Emil, staring open-mouthed at the enormous man. "He's the only fat person I've ever seen."

Jaroslav was on guard immediately. The monsignor wasn't fat, he was huge and very well fed. No one was well fed in Germany after years of war and two hard postwar years with little food.

"Jaroslav Jindrich." The monsignor grabbed his hand and shook it so hard Jaroslav thought his bones might break. "I have a job for you."

"What kind of job?" Jaroslav couldn't take his eyes off the monsignor's enormous stomach. "How do you know who I am?"

"I can pay you well," the monsignor continued. "Come. The waiter here said there was a piece of strudel. Let's go and get it and we'll talk."

Emil's eyes widened in disbelief. "A strudel?"

"They call it that. It's just flour, yeast with some apples and a bit of sugar if we're lucky."

What's the harm in having my first strudel in seven years? Jaroslav thought as he and Emil took their seats in the dining room. But Jaroslav was still suspicious.

"A priest here at St. Cecilia's told me he'd heard of a young man who did excellent sketches and was attempting some paintings. Do you know Father Braun?"

Jaroslav shook his head. "Do you live in Nuremberg?" he asked. In a country full of starving people,
the monsignor looked as if he'd never seen a war.

"I live way up in the mountains, near where I was
born. I have my parish there." He settled his huge bulk
back in his chair, which creaked ominously.

"You must have lots of food up in the mountains," Emil piped up as he licked the last crumb
from his plate.

"We grow our own vegetables at the rectory and
the parishioners provide me with anything I need."
He smiled, patting his enormous stomach. "It's a
healthy life."

"What do you want from me?" Jaroslav spoke
sharply.

"I had to have new furniture made for myself. You
can see why." He patted his stomach again. Then he
leaned close to Jaroslav. "I want you, Jaroslav
Jindrich, to come and hand-paint the tiny folk art
flowers that are so famous as decoration in this
district. You've seen them, *ja*? This form of decorating furniture is hundreds of years old."

He leaned back and Jaroslav winced, hoping the
chair wouldn't collapse. The monsignor lit a cigar.
"You'll come and stay with me. I'll pay you well.
You'll eat fresh vegetables every day, maybe a fish
now and then. I want an artist. You're the one."

A slow smile spread over Jaroslav's face. That'll
be a snap, he thought. They're not even real paintings. And I'll get a holiday! A holiday in the
mountains! No more scratching for food. A chance
to paint . . . "I'll do it," he said.

"But you've never — "

"Shut up, Emil," Jaroslav punched the boy lightly on his upper arm. "Just shut up. What time do we leave?" he asked the monsignor.

"Tomorrow morning. We go by train, then hike up the mountains. With your skill, you should be finished decorating the furniture in two weeks. See you at the station at seven tomorrow."

They shook hands, and Jaroslav hustled Emil through the hotel lobby. The moment they were outside, Jaroslav leaped into the air and shrieked, "A holiday!"

"Do you know how to paint those little flowers, Jaroslav?"

"Sure. It looks easy. Anyone can do that."

Jaroslav ambled along trying to remember what he'd read about this ancient art of decorating. Emil kept glancing up at him, but he wasn't about to tell Emil he just remembered it was more difficult than it appeared. Can I really do it? he wondered. I don't even have any paints.

"Nuts!" he suddenly said. "I want a holiday and I'm going to get a holiday. Come on, Emil, step on it."

Jaroslav hid the noodles in his garret when they got back. He grabbed some more money. "See you tonight," he called to Emil on his way out again. I've got to find someone to show me this craft, he thought as he walked along. He snapped his fingers suddenly — Fräulein Elten. She's been in Nuremberg forever. I bet she knows someone. An hour later Jaroslav was knocking on her door.

"*Nein*," she answered. "That's a special technique." She watched as Jaroslav, a glum look on his face, left her front walk.

"Wait!" she cried, and he stopped. "I just remembered. A pupil of mine told me she saves money to buy a little oil paint for her grandfather. Try him. I'll get the address. Maybe he knows someone."

A little while later, Jaroslav handed over to the elderly gentleman one of his sketches done on the spot.

"You're talented," the man said, turning them slightly this way, slightly that. "All right. I'll show you what I know."

All afternoon Jaroslav sweated to learn the ancient ways of holding the brushes and using the oil paint. The man took the time to show him shortcuts and how to mix the colours. When Jaroslav felt he couldn't learn one more thing, the man wiped his hands on an old rag smelling of turpentine and said, "There. I've given you a start."

Jaroslav was about to leave when the man gestured towards the baby jars, film cannisters and little tins that held his paints. "You better buy some paint from me. You won't find any up in the mountains."

"I'm lucky to find someone as generous as you," Jaroslav said, shaking the elderly man's hand, clutching a bag of paint jars in the other.

"Yes, I have been generous. But you are a true artist," the man smiled. "*Auf Wiedersehen*."

Emil was waiting for him impatiently when Jaroslav returned to his garret. "Elsbeth's got the water boiling. Where did you hide the noodles?"

Jaroslav drew them out from behind his huge pile of magazines and books, and the two of them went downstairs.

"Where have you been, Jaroslav? Hurry up and open up the noodles. The water's boiling. I'll just set the table. Mama and Papa will be back in a minute. They're in the factory."

Jaroslav ripped open the bag — and staggered back. The disgusting smell of mildew that rose from it nearly made him gag. Emil was busy chattering to Elsbeth about the monsignor and the hotel and the strudel. Jaroslav didn't know what to do. His spinach noodles weren't spinach noodles, just mildewed noodles. Quickly, he emptied the whole bag into the bubbling water.

"What are you doing? We could have saved half of those to cook tomorrow." Elsbeth marched over to the stove and grabbed the spoon to give them a stir. But before she could smell them, Frau Hoffer came back in, followed by her husband.

Jaroslav took back the spoon and stirred and stirred, hoping the smell would go away with the boiling. So far no one had noticed. Emil was still going on and on about what a giant the monsignor was.

"Mama, you sit there. Papa, you sit there." Elsbeth pointed. Emil pulled out his chair and sat down.

"Sit down, Elsbeth," Jaroslav said. "I'll serve the noodles." With his back to them, he sniffed deeply a couple of times as he drained them. So far so good, he thought, turning and dishing them out.

As Elsbeth said a special grace thanking God for

Frau Hoffer's return, Jaroslav said his own special one, praying the family wouldn't notice how rancid his noodles were.

"This is a special treat, Jaroslav," Frau Hoffer said, twirling the noodles round her fork and taking her first bite. A strange expression settled on her face, but she kept chewing and smiling.

Jaroslav glanced at Herr Hoffer who had just told everyone that Jaroslav was a brilliant strategist. He also had a funny look on his face as he chewed.

Elsbeth choked, then smiled, and after chewing very carefully murmured, "I've never had spinach noodles before."

Emil stuffed the biggest forkful into his mouth. Immediately he spewed the whole lot out all over his plate and the table. "These are horrible!" He jumped up to spit some more into the sink. "I'm going to be sick!"

The Hoffers carefully avoided looking at each other and seemed to be examining their plates in fascination.

"I'm sorry." Jaroslav sighed. "I paid for spinach noodles, but they sold me noodles green with mildew."

Frau Hoffer came around the table and kissed Jaroslav on the cheek. "Mildewed fruits and vegetables kept me alive many times. The taste of mildew is the taste of life. I'm going to enjoy my noodles." She walked back to her place and sat down. "The rest of you can do what you like." She took yet another mouthful.

Elsbeth started to giggle, while Herr Hoffer and

Jaroslav smiled. Everyone but Emil ate the noodles.

"The gift of food means the recipient will never
go hungry. Thank you, Jaroslav." Frau Hoffer blew
him another kiss and continued eating.

16

Jaroslav's Accomplishments

I was a slave." Frau Hoffer's voice was low after dinner that night, and she couldn't look at her family. "I was terrified when I was herded onto the train. For five days we were carried, packed like cattle, until we reached the coal mines past Moscow. The barracks were frigid, with swirls of snow on the floor. Three women who had lasted the journey died the first week. I knew I had to get out of those barracks."

Frau Hoffer reached out from her place on the bed and drew Emil onto her lap. "Each day I spoke to the commandant in a different language. One day he asked me if I was educated. I answered him in Russian that I had been lucky to be brought up in Czechoslovakia where we spoke three official languages. The very next day his wife took me into their house to tutor their children. My bones were warm during the day at least."

"Did you live in their house, Mama?"

Frau Hoffer's lips pressed in a hard line. "No. Each night I went back to freeze in the barracks. I had to keep one eye open so I wouldn't lose my blanket."

"What happened next, Mama?" Elsbeth sounded so frightened that Frau Hoffer pulled her close to herself as well.

"The commandant's youngest son was crossing the yard one day when his ball rolled under a cart standing with the horse in harness. He started to crawl underneath. Suddenly the horse spooked. It reared up, rocking the wagon violently. I threw myself on the ground, wriggled underneath and half covered the boy with my body. The horse took off, the cart missing the boy's leg only because I yanked him over. Everyone was shouting. The commandant's wife came running and was told that her son would have been killed if I hadn't saved him. That was when I began sleeping in the shed off their kitchen."

"And that's what saved your life?" Jaroslav asked, offering her some of the real coffee that he had brought back.

"I saved my own life. As long as I cooked and sewed the children's clothes, and tutored them and cleaned, I stayed alive and warm. I ate too. But I was a slave. Just a slave."

"But Mama, how did you get to Nuremberg?"

"The commandant was posted to Berlin. When we got there, the whole family was shocked that the city was divided. I knew you were in Bayreuth, waiting. But I didn't have a passport, I didn't have money. I couldn't get to the American zone. Something in me died. I gave up hope. I taught the children, but I was like a robot."

Emil twisted around to look at her. "How long have you been in Nuremberg?"

"Nearly two years."

"Two years!" Elsbeth looked shocked.

"Two years! Oh, Hildegarde," murmured Herr Hoffer.

"You were here the whole time we were." Emil looked as though he was about to cry. "I told them that so many times."

"The commandant was posted very soon from Berlin to Nuremberg to be an observer at the Nuremberg trials. They needed me to go with them because I spoke German so well. It made it easier for them to find a place to live and get food. So I came here."

Tears began to creep down her cheeks as her voice grew hard with memory. "After the trials they packed up to go home. They didn't want to be bothered taking me with them. The wife said I was unhappy all the time. So they gave me enough to live on for one week and left me on the street."

She struggled not to cry. "A nice American nurse bought me two oranges a week from the PX store to sell on the streets. The money paid for a roof over my head. Otherwise I would have been attacked or hurt. You know how hard it is for a woman alone here."

Taking a final, shuddering breath, she grasped both children tightly to her. "I thought you were all back at the camp. I couldn't think about that. I thought maybe Papa had gotten to Bayreuth, but never you, Elsbeth, and never you, Emil." She started to cry. "It was such a shock to see you. I didn't know you. You've grown so much. I still can't believe it."

The room quivered with joy. Herr Hoffer, his adoring gaze on his wife, said quietly, "If Jaroslav hadn't been an artist, we would never have found you. It's him we have to thank."

"Jaroslav's getting a holiday because he's an artist," Emil piped up. "It's his reward for finding Mama."

"Right. And I leave at seven tomorrow morning." Jaroslav stood and stretched. Then he leaned down to softly kiss Frau Hoffer's cheek. "I'm glad you got away," he said.

Herr Hoffer walked him to the door. "Tomorrow I'm applying for the adoption papers, Jaroslav. By the time you come back, we will be ready to get our visas to emigrate."

The moment the monsignor and Jaroslav arrived at the rectory, he was taken to the parlour. "Here, my boy, turn my furniture into *art!*" the monsignor said, sweeping his hand towards four chairs, a table and a china cabinet.

That won't be so hard, Jaroslav thought. But then the next morning his "holiday" began in earnest. And he wished he'd never heard the word.

The monsignor woke him every day at five o'clock for a vigorous fifteen-kilometre walk. Immediately after that Jaroslav was expected to attend Mass. The breakfast of sausages, eggs and black bread was so enormous that Jaroslav made a pig of himself, and then, because he ate so much, he would nearly fall asleep as he attempted to decorate the furniture.

At lunch he couldn't resist all the fresh vegetables and more sausage, and found himself nodding off at the table. So he had to lie down for a nap every afternoon.

"This is the life," boomed the monsignor, dragging Jaroslav to lift weights and do push-ups as soon as they woke from their naps. Every muscle in Jaroslav's body ached as he went back to his painting again. He couldn't wait to get back to Nuremberg. He'd realized that the monsignor wasn't fat with flab, he was rotund with pure muscle.

Supper was lighter than the other two meals, but the cook prided herself on her plum dumplings and loaded Jaroslav's plate. After supper, Jaroslav was expected to accompany the monsignor on another fifteen-kilometre hike. On Sunday night there was Benediction, although there was hardly a soul in the church except Jaroslav, and sometimes through the week if it was a feast day there would be a special Mass.

At the end of each day the priest would come to look at Jaroslav's work. Jaroslav was nervous the first time and hoped he was doing what the monsignor wanted. But although the man inspected his work carefully, he always said the same thing — "Perfect, my boy, perfect." Then the monsignor would clap him so hard on the back that Jaroslav thought his rib cage would fly right out through the front of his chest. It wasn't long before he realized that although the monsignor knew what he wanted, he knew even less about the art than Jaroslav did.

After the inspection, Jaroslav would be dragged into the monsignor's study to listen to the news on the radio while the whole room filled up with putrid cigar smoke, leaving Jaroslav gasping for breath and staggering off to bed nauseated.

"See you bright and early tomorrow," the monsignor would boom as he picked up his clarinet to go and play jazz in the club in town until two or three in the morning.

Jaroslav wondered if the stylized flowers he was painting looked as dipsy as he felt. "This is a vacation?" he asked himself every single morning as he struggled to put one foot on the floor in the dark.

The two weeks were finally over, and Jaroslav, with dark circles under his eyes, marched down the mountain with the monsignor to catch the train back to Nuremberg.

"Next year I want you to decorate the bedroom furniture," boomed the monsignor as he mangled Jaroslav's hand at the station. "You've done a splendid job. I'll tell everyone about your talent. Too bad you're not a musician. You could have played at the club with me."

Jaroslav folded his money, kissed it and put it in his pocket. As he slumped in his seat, he thanked God he would be in Canada next year. And then, instantly, he fell asleep exhausted.

"Jaroslav? Holy Mary, I thought it was Hercules! Is it really you?" Elsbeth stopped work and came to pinch the muscles in his upper arm.

"Just don't mention the word *vacation*," Jaroslav

said bitterly. He handed her the bag of vegetables and sausages the monsignor had given him as a bonus. "Don't cook any for me. I may never eat again."

"We better lock the door," Herr Hoffer said when he came in from work that night. "I smell fresh peas and carrots." He took off his jacket and hung it up. "I got the adoption papers, Jaroslav. We have to sign them and return them to the lawyer tomorrow."

He coughed, putting his hand to his throat. "Then you and I will go right away to the Canadian Consulate for our visas." He coughed again. "Maybe the priest's vegetables will take away my sore throat."

"We'll sail from Hamburg, won't we, Papa?" Emil was breaking open the pods and chomping on raw peas.

"Yes, *liebchen*. Two men already want to buy our factory." He cleared his throat and went to pour a drink of water. "As soon as we have our visas, we'll book passage to Canada."

"How much will the visas cost?" Jaroslav wondered if he'd saved enough.

"The visa-to-immigrate fee is set by the Canadian government. It won't be much." He coughed again and lay down on the bed. "But the passage from Hamburg will cost more than five-hundred American dollars each."

Frau Hoffer, who had been silent, lay a hand on her husband's forehead. "You're burning. You have fever." She wet a cloth and began to bathe her husband's face.

Jaroslav had been surprised at how much passage to Canada would be. I'll be all right, he thought. I've sold so many paper boxes to soldiers and made money on the black market that I'll have some left over. But I wonder if Herr Hoffer has enough to pay for everyone. Jaroslav knew the court case in Hamburg against Herr Director was still dragging on, and a lawyer's bill came in every month.

"Maybe Jaroslav has to go alone to the Canadian Consulate to get our visas," croaked Herr Hoffer as he rolled over to sleep.

Wednesday came and Herr Hoffer said he was better, but he swayed when he stood up. "We can't go to Canada if the doctor can't give you a clean bill of health," Frau Hoffer said. "Let Jaroslav go for the visas. You stay home and rest."

Jaroslav dressed carefully. He wore a good second-hand shirt with a stiffly starched collar and one of Herr Hoffer's ties. His business suit and his briefcase would give an elegant impression, he hoped. I have to look successful, he thought as he slipped his letters of recommendation into his pocket.

"Good luck, Jaroslav," Herr Hoffer rasped, handing him his own letters as Elsbeth hugged him goodbye.

Frau Hoffer looked so sad that Jaroslav suddenly realized she didn't really expect him to succeed.

"I *will* get our visas," he said firmly to her before he set off.

Jaroslav stared around the outer office of the consulate. The seedy, the downtrodden, the slightly insane were all there ahead of him to apply to go to Canada. Only one other man wore a business suit and looked as successful as Jaroslav did. Jaroslav's heart went out to these beaten-down refugees, who had had fierce experiences and would never recover properly. But he knew he had to steel himself to get the Hoffer visas at any cost. We've got to get out of here or we'll all end up just like these people, he thought.

"I want to see the consul himself," he announced loudly in German to the secretary.

The secretary hardly looked up. "These people are ahead of you. You'll have to wait your place in line."

Jaroslav switched immediately to English. "I have excellent letters of reference here, for both Herr Hoffer and myself. No doubt you have heard of Hoffer Incorporated, Herr Hoffer's large factory? No? We're looking into setting up a branch office in Canada." May God forgive me for my lies, Jaroslav thought as he held out the envelope to the secretary, who looked impressed.

"All right," she responded in English without reading the letters. "Come with me."

The consul, a tall man, rose and shook Jaroslav's hand after the secretary had left. He turned to his interpreter and said, "Ask him if he's here to get a visa to immigrate."

Jaroslav spoke up immediately in English. "Mr. Consul, please dismiss your interpreter. You won't need him. As you can see, I speak English perfectly."

"So you do, son. So you do." He waved the interpreter off, as Jaroslav produced his own letters of reference and those of Herr Hoffer, and requested visas for the whole family.

"Well, Mr. Hoffer, the processing of visas takes a little time, but I'm very impressed that you speak English so well. I guess we could do it today." Jaroslav wished he could jump up and dance a jig. The consul took out the forms and began asking Jaroslav questions and filling in his answers.

However, when he got to Jaroslav's form, he stopped. "Why is your name Jaroslav Jindrich-Hoffer?"

"I've been adopted formally by the family. But I wanted to keep my father's name."

The consul looked thoughtful. "There's a lot of this adoption going on in Germany lately." He shrugged. "Well, your letters of reference are excellent. So I guess it's okay."

Smugly Jaroslav thought, I've done it.

Then the consul asked, "What part of Canada does your family plan on going to?"

Jaroslav crossed his fingers behind his back as he lied again. "Herr Hoffer is an engineer, but he and I have been offered salesmen's jobs in British Columbia." He looked the consul right in the eye. "Some Germans who have a leather factory here and in Hamburg have an office in Vancouver. As soon as I graduate from high school and university, I'm going to work for them."

"Herr Hoffer too?"

"Yes. Even Frau Hoffer if she wants a job." He pointed to Herr Hoffer's letters. "Herr Hoffer will sell his business for a lot of money here in Nuremberg. He's going to use that as capital to start up again in Canada."

The consul smiled while he stared long and hard at Jaroslav, who found himself beginning to fidget. "You are very ingenious, young man. You've covered all the bases. If there are any more at home like you, Canada can use them." He rose and extended his hand.

"Is that it?" asked Jaroslav.

"That's it." The man smiled. "I've signed the forms. Take them with your photographs and the medical reports from your doctor, down the hall. Come back in five days. Your visas to immigrate will be waiting. And good luck!"

Once out of the consul's office, Jaroslav leaped in the air and clicked his heels together. He handed the forms and photos in and raced home.

"We got them!" he yelled, slamming the door to the family's room behind him. "In five days we can pick up our visas to Canada!"

"Papa's sick!" Elsbeth didn't even look at him. "Come out with me right away and find an orange. The doctor said he needs vitamin C."

"Didn't you hear me?" Jaroslav grabbed Elsbeth by the hands and swung her round and round. "We got our visas! We can be on our way to Hamburg next week."

"Good, my boy. Good," croaked Herr Hoffer from the bed, his face as pale as the sheets.

"Canada, here we come," chanted Jaroslav.

"Papa hasn't been eating. He's been vomiting. Jaroslav, we can't go anywhere unless he gets better quickly."

Jaroslav halted and stared at them. Even Frau Hoffer, who hadn't said a word, was acting strangely.

"What's going on here?" he said loudly. "What's the matter with all of you?"

No one said anything. Elsbeth waited at the door for him to go with her to get the orange.

Suddenly Jaroslav understood. The Hoffers had waited so long. They'd hungered for Canada. They were numb. And Herr Hoffer was too sick to know what was really happening. Frau Hoffer had endured so many drastic changes that she couldn't cope with the thought of travelling thousands of kilometres more. *They don't believe it's finally happening*, he thought. He felt sad for them, but he was determined not to let it stop his own joy.

"You stay here, Elsbeth," he said, and he ran outside and down the street. Within an hour he was back with an orange. He cut it into four pieces so the man could suck the juice, and he held Herr Hoffer up by the shoulders. "We're going to book passage for Canada next week, Herr Hoffer, so you'd better get well. No one who's sick gets into Canada. *Get Well!*"

The man nodded and smiled weakly. Jaroslav knew Herr Hoffer had the same driving spirit he did. We'll be booking passage next week, I just know it, he almost said aloud. He hummed all the way back to his room.

Maybe the captain will let me onto the bridge so I can see how they steer the ship, he thought as he fell asleep.

17

An Even Chance

Passage to Canada for five. From Hamburg."
Jaroslav laid the money out on the counter
of the steamship line booking office.

The clerk looked up at him

"What are you smirking about, anyway?"

"You wouldn't understand. It's a private joke."

"Well, maybe you can understand *this* private joke. There is no passage available. Most ships that sail for Canada go from Bremen now, anyway."

It took a moment for the words to sink in. "I beg your pardon?"

"It's simple. We're sold out." The clerk shrugged.

"But you can't be sold out. We've waited all this time. We're all ready to go. Herr Hoffer has even sold his business." Jaroslav felt a knot growing in his stomach.

"Too bad. Canada's taking in refugees. Most of them bought tickets ahead of you. From Hamburg and Bremen, anyway." The clerk gave him a smug smile. "Next, please," he called.

Jaroslav clenched and unclenched his fists as he stood looking at the arrogant clerk. "You mean we can't go to Canada." Even to himself he sounded crushed.

"No. Not from Hamburg or Bremen." The clerk turned to wait on the next customer.

Fumbling, Jaroslav gathered up the American dollars. How am I going to tell them? he wondered. What are we going to do? We can't live. We have no income. How are we going to stay alive?

He was almost out the door when he had a thought. He marched back to the counter and interrupted. "You said Hamburg and Bremen, right? No passage from Hamburg and Bremen?"

"I'm busy with this customer. You'll have to wait, as you can see."

"No, no," the businessman spoke up. "This young man was ahead of me. Look after him. I can wait a few minutes." The man winked at Jaroslav.

The clerk spoke in clipped tones. "I told you. No passage from Hamburg and Bremen."

"I heard you. But what about other ports?"

"Other ports?"

"This steamship must also sail from . . . let me see . . . Copenhagen?"

"No. We don't sail out of Copenhagen." The clerk would not look at Jaroslav and shuffled papers on the counter.

"Rotterdam?" The desperation showed in Jaroslav's voice.

"They sail from Rotterdam," the businessman interjected. "He just told me there are plenty of cabins available from Rotterdam. Aren't there?"

Nodding, the clerk slowly reached for his ticket book. Lips pressed together in anger, he wrote up the five tickets. With shaking hands, Jaroslav handed over the money.

When he picked up the tickets, he knew that the direction of his life had shifted. Everything will be different from this moment on, he thought. He kissed the tickets and put them into his money belt. "Thank you, sir," he said to the businessman, barely refraining from hugging him. "Are you sailing from Rotterdam?"

"Yes, I am, my boy. But not on the date you are."

"Somehow, somewhere, I'll find a way to repay you," Jaroslav blurted, a little embarrassed. "Maybe we'll meet in Canada. *Auf Wiedersehen.*"

Jaroslav's feet were wings and he smiled so much on the way home that everyone smiled back at him, even a stooped-over woman pushing her belongings in a doll's carriage. Holland! he thought. A new adventure!

The family were eating the last bit of the monsignor's sausage when Jaroslav burst in. "I got the tickets!" he yelled. "We're sailing in six days from Rotterdam! We'll be in Canada in *two weeks!*"

"Rotterdam! That means we'll have to go first to Holland!" Herr Hoffer, still hoarse, frowned. "We'll need more money to go from Holland."

"Rotterdam!" Elsbeth wailed. "Why can't we sail from Germany? From Hamburg?"

"Rotterdam!" Frau Hoffer looked thoughtful. "I don't speak Dutch. I hope they speak some English in Holland."

"Whoopee!" Emil jumped up, knocking over his chair. "We're going to Canada! Who cares where we sail from? We're getting out of here! I'm packing right now." He ran to the bed and hauled a cardboard suitcase from under it.

"I thought you'd all be happy!" Jaroslav said. "There were no tickets left from Hamburg. We have to go now. If we wait, Canada might not have room for us."

"Jaroslav's right." Herr Hoffer pushed his plate away. "Even though we have our visas, because there are five of us we might get turned back unless we move fast. We can't afford to wait until space turns up from Hamburg."

"Why are you so upset, Elsbeth? We planned on going next week anyway."

"I don't know, Jaroslav. First we were in Czechoslovakia. Then at the hospital it was like we were in the United States. Now we're in Germany. And before we can get out of here, we have to go to Holland. It's easier to sail from Hamburg."

Jaroslav turned away. He couldn't bear to look at any of them, huddled together in one room, with a tiny cupboard for a kitchen. All they've ever talked about is getting out of here and going to Canada, he thought. That kept us alive when all we had to eat was one piece of bread and some watery

soup. We were set to go next week anyway —
what's happened to them? Sailing from Hamburg
or Rotterdam — what's the difference?

"We don't know what lies ahead, in Holland,
Jaroslav." Herr Hoffer came round the table and
faced the boy. "You're young. For Hildegarde and
me, we planned on starting over in Canada, but
now having to go to a new country first . . . it makes
it harder."

"You've already sold your business! We're just
staying overnight in Holland, that's all!"

"We're going. But now that it's actually happening, we're a little nervous. We have German passports. We might not be welcome in Holland. We all
know how quickly things can go wrong."

"Elsbeth?"

"I'm alone here. I have no friends. But at least
here I might accidentally run into someone I went
to school with that might have escaped too. I'll be
alone in Canada with no friends." Her voice broke.
"And to go out through Holland . . . "

"You can make friends on board the ship." Emil
took her hand. "There'll be lots of kids going to
Canada. Maybe they need friends too."

"Do you really think so, Emil?"

"Yes, I do, Elsbeth." Jaroslav patted her shoulder. "Come on, we've saved, worked and starved
to get to Canada. The Holland American line has
huge ships. There's got to be one girl on board
you'll like." He sighed. "I'm the one who'll be
alone, once we sail."

"You're right." Elsbeth smiled and wiped away

her tears. "You've been so brave about leaving your father. I'll pack now too. Maybe I'll even like Holland."

Frau Hoffer came and put her arms around her daughter. "I'm the mother now. You can be a real teenager for a change."

Herr Hoffer put on his jacket to go back into the factory. "The new owners are arriving soon and I'm going to show them some of the last details. We have to allow enough time in case there's a delay on the train to Holland."

"We have to have enough Dutch guilders to stay in Holland longer in case there's a delay in sailing," Elsbeth pointed out.

"We have to eat in Holland too," Emil added.

"That's the spirit," smiled Jaroslav. "Canada, here we come. Come on — all together now: *Canada, here we come.*" Five hopeful voices cheered in unison.

"Passports, please." The uniformed man stood swaying just inside their compartment door. The conductor stood beside him.

The quick smell of fear momentarily filled the grimy compartment, then Herr Hoffer smiled, producing the documents, and everyone relaxed.

"Is this Holland?" asked Emil.

"What do you think, little one?" The conductor twirled a small ticket-punch in his hand. "Is there any other land as flat as this in the whole of Europe?"

Emil squirmed around and peered out the window as the train swayed on towards Rotterdam and the Atlantic Ocean.

Jaroslav wondered how a country could eat, growing flowers. He was tired. The last few days had been hectic as Herr Hoffer rounded up as much money as he could get from the new owners. Jaroslav was dismayed that he had received only a pittance himself for his precious seven books that he had had to sell.

Fräulein Elten had thrown a going-away party, with nothing as elaborate as ham, but she had made a fake strudel and they had all danced a final Strauss waltz together. "I will never again have friends like you," she sobbed when it came time to say goodbye.

Frau Hoffer comforted her. "We'll write. When we start our business in Canada, we'll send you some money towards your passage. You can join us." But they all knew in their hearts that Fräulein Elten was not too likely to come.

Elsbeth and Emil had been in charge of packing the cardboard suitcases. Since they had so few clothes, it was easy. On the day of departure they left the room behind the factory, standing briefly in the doorway, shaking loose the last scent of mould, and dashed across the factory and up the stairs.

Jaroslav had been in charge of rounding up enough food for the journey and had managed to get five bottles of pop at the American PX to spring open once they got into their train compartments. He also bought bread and garlic sausage, which he figured would keep for two weeks at least.

But it all seemed to pass like a slow-motion dream, and now finally they were rolling over this tiny, neat country, where in the spring the sweet smell of hyacinths replaced manure.

"These are real farms," the conductor pointed. "But did you know that some Dutchmen get rich selling thousands of bulbs all over the world?"

"Don't they have to grow food?" Emil asked.

"These farms grow food. The big fields to the west grow red, yellow, white and pink tulips every spring."

At last the train rolled into the station at Rotterdam. One of the porters directed them down towards the harbour. "Get rooms in one of the cheap seamen's pensions," he said, pulling out a map and tracing the route. "You'll be on this side of the river, but you can get a tram across the bridge to the docks. The harbour's across the river."

Everyone was tired and slightly on edge. They were jostled by sailors of every nationality as they walked deeper and deeper into the old district of Rotterdam.

Jaroslav had never seen such narrow houses. He chose one that looked clean, and after receiving a nod from Herr Hoffer, yanked the bell-pull.

"Come on up," boomed a man from the top of a staircase so steep it was like a ladder. "Six guilders for each room. Come." He led the way up yet another steep staircase to two tiny rooms on the top floor. A narrow watercloset was between them. "Go the pub next door for meals," he said as he collected his money and left.

Elsbeth pulled the two murphy beds down in one

room, and there was no place left to stand. She
crawled onto one and lay with her hands behind
her head. "No bedbugs, anyway," she yawned as
Frau Hoffer lay down beside her.

In the other room, Herr Hoffer, Jaroslav and
Emil pulled down their beds and also rested. Emil
fell asleep almost instantly.

"Herr Hoffer?" Jaroslav whispered. "Are you
scared? About leaving, I mean."

"We've burned our bridges behind us, Jaroslav.
We're totally cut off now. In Germany it was awful
but we spoke the language, I had business friends,
we were all poor. In Canada, we'll be all alone.
Most people have jobs. But we don't. We'll have
no money after the first month."

"I'm scared too." Jaroslav propped himself up
on one elbow. "But Canada is rich. No one dropped
any bombs on Canada."

Just then they heard the bell-pull yanked almost
off its rope and heavy steps came up the stairs.
There was a hard knocking at their door. Jaroslav
jumped up to open it, his heart in his throat.

"Passports!" demanded the policeman from
Interpol who stood at their door. Jaroslav and Herr
Hoffer scrambled to get them. Across the hall, Frau
Hoffer and Elsbeth peeked out, looking terrified.

Coldly the policeman examined the documents,
checked their photographs, then pocketed them all.
"Pick them up tomorrow at the police station,
before you sail." Then he left.

Jaroslav waited until the outside door had
slammed behind the policeman. "In Canada, the

police don't stop you on the street and take away your passport, do they?"

"No." Herr Hoffer was angry too. "It's because we're poor. Before the war a thing like this would never have happened to us. We would have stayed at a decent hotel. It's because we're staying down at the harbour where all the seamen stay."

"But I bet in Canada they don't take poor people's passports away just because they're staying at a harbour." Jaroslav was amazed at the passion he felt.

He threw his murphy bed into the wall. "Come on, Emil. Come on, everybody. Let's go next door for some *olie bollen*. I saw a sign."

"What's *olie bollen?*"

"Little doughnuts, I think." Jaroslav led the way down the stairs and out onto the cobblestoned street.

"Let's eat first. Then we can walk along the river. Maybe we can look across and see our ship." Elsbeth grabbed Emil's hand.

Jaroslav walked shoulder to shoulder with Herr Hoffer. It was the fall again. Everything important to us has happened in the fall, he thought.

"Remember, Herr Hoffer, when you told us the gateway to Canada was through Nuremberg and then we got there and the city was bombed out? It was tough, but you got us a roof over our head and you started your factory."

He paused and turned to face the older man. "Going to Canada is different. We'll have an even chance there. The *SS Ryndam* is the gateway to Canada today, Herr Hoffer. Canada means freedom. We're going to be okay."

18

Freedom

J aroslav stared up at 11,000 tonnes of gleaming
ocean liner as he followed the family up the
gangway. "It's as long as a soccer field," he said.
"The *SS Ryndam* is a floating city."

They handed their tickets to the officer standing
at the top, then followed a crew member along the
outside deck, down the wide staircase to their tiny
inside cabins, side by side and across the hall. They
were perspiring and nervous, since they all had had
to go downtown to the central police station to pick
up their passports before taking the tram across the
bridge to the docks.

"I want the upper bunk." Emil scrambled up into
it. Jaroslav felt as though he was in a doll's cabin.
There was a tiny basin, no porthole, a few centimetres of floor space and the bunks.

But the steward quickly turned on the fan to
circulate the air. "It's small, sir, but you won't be

spending much time in your cabin. There is shuf-fleboard on the upper deck, games every night in the lounge, a library, a duty free shop and" — he hesitated — "if you're feeling tough, there's still water in the swimming pool, but the ocean wind can be cold."

Emil's eyes were large as ponds as the steward listed the menus in the two restaurants. "Depend-ing on your preference, sir, we have chicken, roast beef, sometimes fish, fresh carrots, potatoes, toma-toes, all kinds of cheeses and pâtés." He smiled up at Emil. "And of course, cakes, pies, strudels, candies and fruit."

By this time Herr and Frau Hoffer and Elsbeth, who had seen their own cabins, stood in the door-way listening. No one said a word. They simply stared at the steward, their achingly thin bodies in threadbare clothes contrasting with his well-fed one, bulging in white linen and gold braid.

"We sail tonight at seven," the steward contin-ued. "Nothing on board will be open until then. The first dinner sitting is at seven-thirty. There is a second one at nine-thirty."

He seemed to find it difficult to look right at them. He finally blurted out, "There's lots of food. The bar is also equipped to serve snacks. It's included in your passage." He repeated, "There's lots of food. If you eat too much . . . I mean, if you get sick from eating too much . . . we have our own doctor and nurse on board." Then he dashed from the room.

Everyone just stood there. Food, Jaroslav

thought. People are going to give us food. All the food we want. We don't have to walk for hours to get it. Even carrots. Even chicken . . . They're not going to charge us more and more for it. He turned away as he felt the tears come, and sat down on his bunk.

When he looked up, he could see that the Hoffers, still standing at the doorway, were also struggling with the idea of food for the asking.

"Seven years," he said aloud. The others nodded. "Seven years of no food." He jumped up and pushed past them into the hall. "It's over! It's over!" he cheered, grabbing Elsbeth by the hands and whirling her in an awkward dance in the narrow hall. Laughing, Emil jumped down to join them. The Hoffers stood watching as all up and down the hall doors opened silently and other bone-thin refugees, neat, smelling clean and looking scared, peeked out. "It's over," Jaroslav finally sighed, collapsing against the wall. "It's over."

"Come. Unpack now, children. Then we can go up and watch them cast off from Rotterdam."

Elsbeth lingered to say a few words to Jaroslav but was interrupted by the steward. "Miss Hoffer? This is your roommate, Miss Kuhun." He opened their cabin door, explained again about the ship's routine and left.

The girl hadn't said a word. She stared at Elsbeth and Jaroslav with terrifyingly hollow eyes.

"My name is Elsbeth. What's yours?"

"Eva." Her voice was so low Jaroslav had to lean forward to hear it.

"We're going to Halifax. Are you?"

The girl nodded, then entered the tiny cabin. She hesitated, turned and walked back down the hall the way she had come.

Elsbeth frowned, then ran after her. "Eva?" she called. The girl stopped and Elsbeth caught up to her. "I was in a camp too," she said quietly.

The girl stared at Elsbeth as if waiting for something. "Let's go and play shuffleboard. Would you like that, Eva?" The girl nodded, and Elsbeth waved to Jaroslav. "See you up top at seven."

Jaroslav shivered, leaning over the railing in the crisp fall air, that evening. Whistles blew all around him as the cables were cast off, and everyone but him and the Hoffers waved goodbye to people on the dock. Everything important to us happens in the fall, he thought again. The escape, the trip to Hamburg and now sailing for Canada.

Holy Mary, full of grace, he prayed silently. Look after my father. Let him stay alive. Let me see him again.

Jaroslav's eyes overflowed as he glanced at the Hoffers, standing silently beside him, bathed in the smell of smoke from other freighters and the bite of salt from the sea.

There was nothing to say. Frau Hoffer bit her lip, and Herr Hoffer was also forcing back tears. Jaroslav felt he knew the emptiness the man felt at leaving the familiar way of making a go of things, however poor.

"We're leaving forever," Elsbeth murmured.

It was all too much for Jaroslav as friends on

board hurled colourful paper streamers at friends on the dock. "I'm hungry. Let's get ready for dinner," he said loudly.

At seven-thirty, bathed and dressed, the family took the elevator up to the enormous dining room. Standing on the thick carpet under chandeliers of Italian glass, Herr Hoffer straightened, and in spite of the worn cuffs on his suit, before their very eyes he became again the man of wealth that he had been at home. His bearing, the manner in which he expected and got the best table by the window from the maitre d', were new to Jaroslav, whose own father had originally been one of Herr Hoffer's employees.

But when the waiter brought the menus, with appetizers, soups, three entrées, vegetables and an endless choice of desserts, Jaroslav noticed Herr Hoffer's hands shaking as much as those of the rest of the family.

"No appetizer. No soup," Herr Hoffer said firmly.

"But Papa . . . ," Emil pouted.

"We'll get sick if we eat too much rich food. Papa's right."

Elsbeth sounds like her mother, thought Jaroslav.

They all ordered just one entree. Everything was formally served by waiters wielding forks and spoons, dishing the meat and vegetables onto their heated gold-rimmed dinner plates. Jaroslav fingered the white linen tablecloth as the aroma of gravy, chicken, potatoes, peas and stewed tomatoes filled his nostrils.

When the waiter asked if they would like dessert, there was no holding anyone back. Even Herr Hoffer, in spite of what he'd said, ordered torte as well as applecake, and Jaroslav added ice cream to that. They finished their meal off with real coffee.

As they strolled along the deck, breathing in the sea air, shyly but formally greeting the other D.P.s and the Americans who were going home, Jaroslav knew this was his real vacation. And he made up his mind to enjoy it.

Later that night, he and Emil bet on a giant horse race, with figures about half a metre long, organized by the steward in the main lounge. Then Herr Hoffer insisted that they all, even Emil, go dancing to the small orchestra in the main lounge.

At one in the morning, as he finally tucked Emil into his upper bunk, Jaroslav knew he was truly happy. I'll never have a time like this again, he thought as he climbed into bed. He fell asleep smiling.

The next day the family fell into shipboard routine as if they were born to it. They had breakfast, strolled on the promenade, had coffee, read, had lunch — and by this time Jaroslav was bored and restless.

"Come on, Emil, let's visit the engine room."

"The signs say the engine room is out of bounds, Jaroslav. We can't go there."

"We never know until we try. Maybe one of the crew members might let us take a look."

Off they went, asking directions and going down, down into the bowels of the ship. As the noise grew louder, Jaroslav knew they were almost there.

"Please, sir," he asked a man in overalls. "We want to go into the engine room and take a look."

"Out of bounds," the man said, pulling open a door that Jaroslav could see led to a catwalk. Just as he stepped through it, he turned and winked. "But who would know if two boys just stepped in and stood right here and watched."

The heat was a blanket that stifled them as they stepped onto the catwalk to look over the railings, down onto engines three stories high. Fascinated, they watched as the giant pistons plunged up and down in the immaculately clean cavern. The man who had let them in climbed down a long ladder and began oiling several of the engines.

"That looks like fun. I wish I could do it," Emil breathed.

They watched for over an hour, until the man who had spoken to them came up the ladder and along the catwalk. "Big storm brewing. Better get back to your cabins."

"Let's go up to the very top and see." Emil was off and running. Outside, as they mounted the stairs, they found it was dark. High waves washed steadily over the lower wooden decks.

"Hang onto those ropes they've strung along the railings," Jaroslav shouted as the wind began its eerie howling through the funnels. Then he took off his belt and looped it through Emil's to hold onto him. They both slipped twice as they went up and up to each higher deck.

"Look! That one must be at least fifteen metres high." Emil pointed as the wave rose and rose, then crashed diagonally against the *Ryndam*. Then the rain came, striking hard against their faces.

"Are we going to sink, Jaroslav?" Emil sounded as though it would be a real adventure.

"Don't be silly. Passenger liners don't sink unless they're torpedoed or something fails."

Jaroslav was startled to find a steady stream of other passengers coming up behind them, also making their way to the very top deck. "Why are you going up to the promenade?" he asked an elderly couple, who slid and almost fell.

"If you can keep your eyes on the horizon, my boy, you won't get seasick." The man staggered on.

"There's an elevator," Jaroslav yelled after him. "It would be easier for you."

"An elevator is the worst place to be in a storm," shrieked another refugee, clinging to the rope. "Stairs are bad too."

Drenched through, Emil and Jaroslav hauled their way along the ropes. It seemed to Jaroslav that the captain had altered course to broach the waves more with the bow. This eased the swaying and listing, but as the ship plunged into the gully and Jaroslav saw a huge wave ahead, he found the ship crested the waves and managed to keep on top.

Suddenly his legs went out from under him and he plunged, tugging Emil after him. "Here now, you boys should be with your parents." A crew member had grabbed them just as they were falling. "Go back to your cabins."

"I don't want to go back," Emil yelled after the crewman had gone. "Mama and Papa might be up top on the promenade. Let's go and see." Giving in, Jaroslav led the way again.

At last they reached the enormous open top deck. Ringing the rails of the plunging-rising ship were dozens and dozens of refugees, hanging on for dear life and all of them staring hard, straight ahead at the horizon. All around them the Atlantic Ocean played with the ship as if it were a toy, tossing it this way and that.

"Mama and Papa aren't here," yelled Emil, who had been busy looking up and down the deck. "Let's go back, I'm feeling sick."

On the trip back to their cabins the crew were ever present, reassuring everyone that no one had ever been washed overboard from a passenger liner. But Jaroslav found that just as he would go to put his foot down, the ship would ride down into the gully of a wave. In the end he sat down and told Emil to do likewise. "We'll bump down the stairs on our backsides."

They reached the door to the inside stairwell. But the ship rose and fell so much that Jaroslav began to feel sick too.

Emil managed to get to the hall and then slipped and fell, hitting his head. "Mama!" he shrieked.

"Emil!" a faint voice answered.

Jaroslav helped him to his feet and into the cabin, pushing him into the upper bunk. "Hang on and try to sleep. I'm going to see if your parents are okay."

When he opened the door of the Hoffers' cabin

he found both of them had been sick. Frau Hoffer looked green and Herr Hoffer was unable to get up. "Where's Elsbeth?" he gasped.

"I'll see." Jaroslav knocked on Elsbeth's door, where he found her calmly reading to Eva. "Are you sick?" he asked. She shook her head and Jaroslav returned to his own cabin, hoping his own seasickness would not get worse.

All through that dreadful night, the ship heaved up and down in rhythm with Jaroslav's stomach, and the wind howled. When he wasn't being sick, Emil was.

By midmorning the next day the ship began to stabilize, and the stewards come around knocking on doors asking if passengers would like some tea. Jaroslav lay like a dead man until that night and then crawled up on deck to get some air. Emil slept, and there was no sign of the Hoffers. He suspected Elsbeth had probably played checkers or read through the whole storm.

As the sea calmed the following day, they all looked forward to their second-last night's sleep on board a ship that would remain stable. After that some passengers appeared cheery at the dining room and even snacked on some food.

But Jaroslav wanted to be off the Atlantic Ocean. I can't wait until we get to Canada, he thought. As soon as I get some money saved to try to bring my father over, it's riding the rails, sketching and writing for me. I may never set foot on a ship again, and as for vacations — who needs one?

As the SS Ryndam approached Nova Scotia, the

Hoffers and Jaroslav watched as passing freighters hooted and the boats fishing for cod and halibut blew their whistles. They shielded their eyes against the horizon for a glimpse of Halifax harbour.

What if I'm sent back? What if all of us are sent back? Jaroslav knew the Hoffers were afraid too. All of them had learned not to trust anything when their lives were held in the hands of the authorities. Yet, excited, all of them leaned over the railing looking for a roof, a chimney, a spire.

"What's that white building on that hill?" Emil pointed.

"That's the Citadel," a steward said in passing. "It has the Canadian ensign flying above it."

Jaroslav shivered in the chilly fall air as the pilot boat brought immigration officials on board. "They'll set tables up on one of the outside promenades, sir," a waiter told them. "Everyone has to present themselves and their credentials first to them, then again at Pier 21, where we dock."

The tugs had now come out and threw their lines to the *SS Ryndam* to lead the ship into dock.

The family stared at the new world of freedom.

Why doesn't it look new and shiny? Jaroslav thought. Aloud he said, "Canada looks . . . different."

"It doesn't look rich at all. It looks poor." Emil was staring at the houses and churches and graveyards that dotted the hills rising from the harbour, up to the Citadel.

"There are a lot of black evergreen trees, aren't

there?" Herr Hoffer picked Emil up to comfort him, but he looked glum too.

The family passed the first inspection by the Canadian immigration officials. The gangway was lowered, and confused and frightened again, the Hoffers carried their modest cardboard suitcases down to the pier.

Inside the noisy hall of Pier 21, hundreds of passengers huddled in small groups. Some were obviously penniless and didn't speak the language. "Look, there's Eva," said Elsbeth and ran to give her friend a hug. But Eva shrank back and buried her face in her mother's dress.

Jaroslav now felt lost, and he knew the Hoffers felt the acute despair that followed every passenger. In my dreams I was going to leap off the ship and kiss the ground of Canada. But now, I don't know . . . Maybe Canada is a poor country, he thought.

"Can we help you?" Two elderly women smiled at the Hoffers. "We're from the Travellers' Aid. We're here to assist you. Oh, you speak English. Well, you'll be fine. Here's the name of a good cheap restaurant and this is a list of clean rooming houses in the downtown area. These people run honest houses. They won't cheat you."

"It's a good thing we had a little vacation," Jaroslav said. "We'll have to work harder here than in Nuremberg."

But Elsbeth had been examining the dock and the pier and listening to the announcements and the conversations of the Sisters of Service, who were also there to help. "There are no soldiers with rifles and bayonets here, ready to fire. There's only one policeman and he's smiling," she pointed out. "Nobody looks as if they're starving."

She's right, Jaroslav thought, silently thanking her for getting them all back on track to pursue their dream. "Herr Hoffer, you called me a man of strategy. Let's go to the church and light a candle of thanks that we got here safely. Then we should kneel and gather some of the free earth of Canada. We'll keep it in an envelope. We have escaped to freedom. The earth will always remind us of that."

That night they ate dinner in the restaurant the Travellers' Aid had recommended.

"Who would ever believe our first meal in Canada would be egg rolls, chicken chow mein and honey garlic shrimp balls?" Elsbeth laughed, looking around the Chinese restaurant.

"Tomorrow morning," Herr Hoffer said, "I'm going to make an appointment with the director of the largest bank in Halifax. Jaroslav, you'll come too. We'll decide whether we should stay here or go on by train to Montreal or Toronto."

"We're together, we're free and we've got enough to live on for one month," Jaroslav said. "We're going to be all right. Isn't that so, Herr Hoffer? Frau Hoffer? Elsbeth? Emil?"

Historical Note

*E*scape to Freedom is the story of a family who flees Czechoslovakia, across No Man's Land, to safety in West Germany, and from there, eventually, to Canada. Their adventures, triumphs, fears and heartbreaks characterize the great immigration of Europeans to Canada in the late 1940s and early 1950s, following the Second World War.

At one time, the town of Saaz, where the Hoffer family lived, was in Bohemia, a province of Austria, in Europe. Elsbeth's and Emil's parents, grandparents and great-grandparents were Austrians who never thought of being anything else. But in 1918, at the end of the First World War (often called the Great War), the province of Bohemia was taken away from Austria by the Allies (who had won the war) to become part of a brand-new country, named Czechoslovakia.

This new country was made up of three provinces, Bohemia, Moravia and Slovakia, with three different peoples, each with their own language. The former Austrians spoke German (like Elsbeth and Emil); the Czechs spoke Czech — the main language of the new country (like Jaroslav); and the Slovaks spoke Slovak, which is similar to Czech. Each province tried to keep its own language and customs, and the people of the new country did not always understand one another. Of course, some Czechs lived in the German-speaking part of this new country, and some people spoke or understood more than one language, like Jaroslav.

The new country of Czechoslovakia became a true democracy in 1918, and all political parties — including the Communist Party — had a say in the nation's government until 1939, the beginning of the Second World War. Germany crossed the border and invaded Czechoslovakia; it declared the German-speaking provinces (where Elsbeth, Emil and Jaroslav lived) part of Germany, and the rest of the country was declared a German protectorate.

In 1945, at the end of the Second World War (when *Escape to Freedom* begins), Czechoslovakia was liberated by the Russian army. At that time, Russia was on the same side as Canada, England and the United States, all of them allies against Germany. *But it was not the same Czechoslovakia.* The moderate people who tried to re-establish the country as a democracy — like Elsbeth's father —

were suppressed. More and more communists took over, sometimes aided by Czech veterans who had spent the war years in Russia. Behind the scenes, Russia and the KGB under Stalin were plotting to take over as much of Europe as possible. In a few short months, the communists managed to seize more and more power, and Czechoslovakia became a communist country, run by the people in the country who had belonged to the Communist Party. The famed Iron Curtain dropped.

On June 6, 1945 (when *Escape to Freedom* begins), just months after the end of the Second World War, the German minorities were expelled from the country regardless of their political beliefs or whether their ancestors had homesteaded hundreds of years before. This was called "Being Disowned." Many of these people were arrested without warning and thrown into huge makeshift camps. By government edict, the German-speaking people had all their possessions — such as their houses and cars, or the factory owned by Elsbeth's father — taken away from them. How closely this law was enforced depended on how strict the local Communists and the police wanted to be.

People lucky enough not to be thrown into camps fled penniless, without food and with very few belongings, to West or East Germany. They joined more than 20 million refugees (close to the total population of Canada today), all trying to make a new start in the midst of the bombed ruins of a defeated Germany. But Germany, a country a little larger than southern Ontario, didn't want them. These were the Displaced Persons (D.P.'s), people without a country, who immigrated to Canada in the late 1940s and 1950s, immeasurably enriching Canada.